Music of My Heart

An Inspirational
Christmas Romance

Sophia Isaac

CUT TO THE CHASE PRESS

Sophia Isaac/Cut to the Chase Press
San Antonio, Texas U.S.A.
www.cuttothechasepress.com

Publisher's Note: This is a work of fiction. The characters, places, and events are fictitious. Any resemblance to actual people, living or dead, is coincidental and not intended by the author.

Cover art by Melody Simmons

Music of My Heart/ Sophia Isaac. -- 1st ed.
Ebook Edition ISBN 978-1-949730-00-5
Paperback Edition ISBN 978-1-949730-01-2

Dedication

To my mother, who spent most of her adult life focused on raising her children alone, and who never remarried in part because she didn't understand what Jesus meant about divorce until too late for it to make a difference in her life. We appreciated every sacrifice she made for us— but I wish she had allowed herself the joy of marrying again.

I love and miss you, Mom.

Miss you every day.

And to my adorable husband: I didn't know how good life could be until I met you.

Thank you for transforming my world and for loving me just as I am.

Acknowledgments

No writer creates in isolation. Many thanks to all my friends at San Antonio Romance Authors who have helped and supported me along the way. Special thanks to Willa Blair and Suanne Schafer, fellow authors who read an early version of this book, and Deborah, good friend and smart cookie who helped me fine tune it.

Your support means the world to me.

Contents

Chapter One

Sleigh bells ri-i-i-ing, are you listenin'?

"No, I'm not listening!" Alyson plugged her ears and grimaced. "If I hear this song one more time, I'm going to scream!"

"At least it's a classic." Barbara shut the receipt tape cover on the cash register. "It's better than that hip-hop version of 'Silent Night' that plays every hour."

"No kidding. Mall workers should unite for a torture-free workplace during the holidays." Alyson marked the time on her clipboard and noted that all was shipshape for the opening hour. She smiled fondly at the older woman who'd been called from another store to cover Alyson's department. "I sure wish all my staff were as good as you, Barb. At least I know housewares isn't falling to pieces while I'm out playing Mrs. Claus."

Alyson flipped on the cash-wrap light. The only thing now was to open the chain gate to let in the customers already lined up for doorbuster deals.

"Don't you worry, hon, I've got this covered. You make sure that delinquent Santa doesn't have booze on his breath this morning. You see the news?"

"Are you kidding? We broke the Internet with our drunk Santa. I'm surprised I didn't lose my job. If Mr. Giles himself hadn't hired him, I bet I would've been fired. What a disaster." Alyson sighed and resisted sharing more. Barbara was a temporary, so it wasn't practical to get too attached.

Alyson was too busy to chat anyway. She had a show to run and employees to manage and only—she checked her watch—thirty seconds before the store opened. "Doors opening, Barb." Then louder, to her trusted Linens manager down the hall, "Hector, doors!"

Alyson jogged to the security box, plugged in her code, and the chain gate whirred into life with a jingle, rising slowly.

Impatient customers crouched low to get under the gate before it rose even halfway. Once one person did it, everybody rushed in, bending under the gate, jostling each other, trying to make sure they were in position to get the best deals before anyone else.

Every Christmas, decent folk turned into complete jerks, competing to buy the hottest or most expensive gifts. She hated Christmas.

Especially now. First year as a divorcée. First year providing Christmas for her boys by herself. First year she was not only working overtime but almost double-time since she'd been put in charge of Santa's Wonderland.

The original event planner had quit after only a week when their first Santa broke his leg and canceled on them. Then the boss hired his out-of-work brother-in-law to be Santa, even though he had no prior experience, and had delegated the whole thing to Alyson. The new Santa had gotten rip-roaring drunk on the job, his water bottle filled with cheap bourbon. Disaster.

Those poor kids! Alyson had shut down the line as soon as she'd understood the problem, but it was too late, and parents were royally peeved. She would be, too, if it had happened to her boys. No child should have to recoil from Santa's alcohol breath and be told "Ya get whatcha get, and ya don't throw a fit!"

She had wanted to shut down the whole operation, but Mr. Giles had said, "Never end on misery. That is all people will remember you for. We push forward."

Great advice and very inspirational to hear—unless you are suddenly the one planning everything. She'd spent the rest of the day on the phone securing a new Santa from an actors' agency and dealing with angry parents. Her floor manager duties pushed to after hours.

She'd come home too late to tuck her sons into bed, something she'd promised herself would never happen—they would always come first. And then she'd cried in the bathroom, hiding from her mother's blaming tone.

But today would be better. It had to be better. *Put on a smile, Alyson. A smile is your most important accessory.* She couldn't get Mr. Giles's voice out of her head.

She straightened the floor signage the rushing people had knocked askew, helped an elderly couple shuffling in find the department they wanted, and then quick-stepped it down the long hall to meet with the new Santa before Santa's Wonderland opened.

The way was clear, so she closed her eyes and took a deep breath as she walked, attempting the One-Minute Mindfulness Meditation from the video Mr. Giles forced all the managers to watch. She focused on the smart and efficient *tock-tock* sound of her shiny Mary Jane heels filling the hallway, all other sounds distant as most stores were yet to open.

What an empowering sound her heels made. Smart. Tough. Capable. She wished she felt as confident as they sounded.

"Nice shoes, Ms. Stefanelli."

Startled, she almost slipped as she turned to the deep voice behind her. Marcus, the Ginormous Elf. He was so handsome, his amber eyes a warm surprise against his dark brown skin. Even casual, in a t-shirt and jeans, he looked amazing. At least when he was wearing his ridiculous elf costume, it was easier to ignore her attraction. She dropped her gaze, hoping he didn't see her interest. There was no time for such foolishness. She was done with men, and he was just another temporary employee for the holidays.

He caught up to her, and she kept going, waving for him to walk with her. She barely came to his shoulder, three of her strides to one of his. She didn't slow down.

"Hey, about the schedule. I can't work Sunday."

"Good morning to you, too, Marcus. I'm in a bit of a hurry. I'm meeting with the new Santa."

"Okay, so two issues. I can't work this Sunday. If you don't change it, I'll be a no-show."

"Duly noted. I haven't changed the schedule because I haven't had time. Next issue."

"You've got us all in the wrong positions. I should not be directing traffic, that's not what I signed on for. I was supposed to have the middle position, the entertainer. Or do I not have the right 'look' to talk to people?"

Gut punch. *Ouch*. Alyson stopped and gave him her full attention. "I'm sorry I said that. And I never for a second meant that elves couldn't be African-American, I just meant that you're a big guy and elves aren't built like you."

She glanced at his broad muscular shoulders and chest, then back up to his eyes.

He grinned at whatever he saw on her face.

She cleared her throat. "Anyway, thank you for covering your tattoos and . . . scar."

He cocked his head. "It's an omega. All my frat brothers have it. You thought it was a gang symbol or something? Come on."

"I never said that. It's just . . . creepy."

"How did you even see it? It's over my heart. It's always covered." He tapped the area with his hand, drawing her eye.

Heat crawled up her neck. She picked up the pace again and tried not to look at him, keeping her gaze straight ahead at the escalators still too far away to save her.

"Hey, when did you check me out?"

By the tone of his voice, she could tell he was smiling.

She couldn't walk any faster but avoided his eyes all the same, not willing to explain she had seen Marcus change shirts the first day when the guys opted to finish dressing in the breakroom so the lone girl elf could have privacy.

It had struck her then that not one of them saw her as a woman who might be bothered by this. Clearly, they saw her only as a boss. She knew she wasn't here to make friends, but it still hurt.

And there was the problem that since that day she couldn't get the sight of his bare chest out of her mind. But that sort of happiness was not for her—not now she was divorced. The only reason that she was attracted to Marcus was he resembled her ex. That's it. She was lonely, but she could deal with lonely. Providing for her boys was her number one priority. No distractions.

As she neared the escalators, she peered to the floor below and saw that families were already lining up, and her elves—her crowd control—were nowhere in sight. "Oh, no! Didn't these people see all the bad press?" Taking the stairs rather than the escalator, she went as fast as her heels and pencil skirt would allow.

She stormed into Santa's Workshop behind the stage, the small cabin that acted as their HQ and breakroom.

As soon as Alyson entered, a few of the elves got to their feet and shuffled nervously, waiting for an order. She had that effect on people.

Alyson thumbed behind her. "People are lining up already. I know they're early, but I need two elves to go set up the ropes to keep these people in line and—"

"Why are the ropes down?" the girl elf said. And even though she was the only girl, Alyson still couldn't remember her name. It was a boy's name, like Evan or Devon or something.

"Oh, you weren't here yesterday. The cleaning crew had to replace certain areas where the . . . um . . . vomit . . ." She felt sick just remembering it. Drunk Santa had puked as they led him away, and the kids and parents waiting in line who'd been eating too much candy and drinking too much coffee had reacted in kind. Nastiness. Oh, the smell. "Thank you all for coming back, by the way."

"Hazard pay?" Bertie, the college boy, held out his hand with a comical smile.

"Afraid not. And thanks for volunteering. Explain yesterday to Devon." She glanced at the girl to see if she'd gotten the name right. *Yes!* "Then go fix those velvet ropes and candy canes. Please."

Scanning the room, she realized something wasn't right. She counted. Six elves, there should be eight. "Wait a minute. Other than Marcus, who isn't here yet? And have any of you seen an older gentleman with white hair—"

"And a white beard, in a jolly red suit?" Bertie joked, donning his elf hat and smock.

"Ha ha. We have a new Santa, from an agency this time, but he was supposed to be here waiting for me"—she glanced at her watch—"eight minutes ago."

Bertie and Devon walked out the door, and Alyson followed slowly, scrolling through her contacts on her phone for the agency's number. *Boom!* She ran right into a brick wall. A warm brick wall that smelled divine. Stunned, she staggered back. "I'm so sorry, Marcus, I—" She cut short her apology when she met his gaze and saw the slow smile climbing.

She knew her hot ears were pink but hoped her makeup kept her embarrassment from showing on her cheeks.

He stepped aside, holding the door, and with a flourish of the hand and a bow he said, "Ladies first."

With a deep breath to cleanse her psyche, she passed into the mall and focused on the task at hand. The crowd was growing. Her stomach clenched on the twenty-ounce dark roast she'd consumed for breakfast.

Searching the massive marble hallways to the north, south, east, and west, she grew more worried at the number of shoppers arriving early now that school was out for the holidays. No guys who looked like Santa.

She swallowed the acid in her throat and glanced at her watch again. Fifteen minutes to showtime. Santa was supposed to be here to review the schedule with her. Santa was the star. You can't have Santa's Wonderland with no Santa!

She found the agency in her contacts and placed the call as she hurried back into the workshop. Waiting for the agency to pick up, she surveyed the room to make sure the elves were ready. A few were still putting on their gear.

Marcus, now in green tights and a red-belted green tunic, sat back, reading a book, his legs stretched out before him. Or rather, pretending to read his book—she had seen his eyes flick down to the page. Then he watched her over the top of the paperback again. A well-worn Tolkien. In her mind, he went from potential gang member with all those tats to *Lord of the Rings* nerd in an instant.

He cocked his head at her, questioning. Her belly fluttered, and she looked away. He shouldn't affect her like this now he was dressed as an elf and looked silly. It was like seeing Hercules dressed as a court jester—it was just wrong. But the tights were nice.

She closed her eyes. *Don't do this to yourself, Alyson. Just ignore him.*

The phone connected. "Agency hours are" — *great, a stupid recording—* "Monday through Friday, eight a.m. to five p.m. and Saturday, noon to four p.m."

"Noon? You've got to be kidding me!" She hung up and resisted the urge to throw her phone at the wall.

Focus, Alyson. She took a deep breath and bit her lip to stop herself from crying out of frustration. Another deep breath, then she checked her watch. "Everyone to your places. Stay on script. Santa may be a little late. Stall as best you can."

She left the room to scan the crowd and the hallway for Santa again. No such luck, but she saw her mother and two sons waving wildly at her from the line, all three with big smiles. Alyson waved back and blew a kiss. Her poor boys were going to witness a disaster. No Daddy and no Santa. This Christmas was the worst.

"Ms. Stefanelli, about my position . . ." Marcus appeared beside her.

"No changes. There isn't time." She looked once again into the crowd, the line now stretching beyond the ropes into the hallway. All these families were so desperate for a Christmas experience. An experience she would fail to deliver.

"I'm supposed to be the center elf. I'm good with people, with kids."

She turned her attention to him again. "But we need your strength for lifting kids on and off Santa's lap." She avoided touching him, instead merely glancing at his strong arms. "No one can do that for as long as you can. And two elves didn't show." She looked him in the eye. "I'd give you the center if I could. I'm sorry, Marcus."

She could see the acceptance in his eyes. *Thank goodness*. "Now, please excuse me, I have to go become old before my time."

She ducked back into the workshop and pulled the shapeless red velveteen dress over her own fitted skirt and top, donned the Mrs. Claus white wig and bonnet, and the wire-rimmed glasses.

Swooping out of the workshop and up the steps to the stage, she waved like royalty to the crowd, making an effort to smile at each and every little one who waved back. A glance at her watch as she waved—two minutes behind schedule.

"Welcome! Welcome to Santa's Wonderland! Children and moms, dads, grandparents and everyone! I am Mrs. Claus, and I'm here to let you know Santa is all better today, but he is still busy in the workshop—"

"Drinking!" A man in the crowd hollered. Some people laughed but not many. Most people looked nervous.

"He's making his list and checking it twice before he gets busy adding all of you boys and girls to that list." Her voice sounded fake and saccharine sweet even to her own ears. "It will just be a few minutes before we get started. In the meantime, the elves will help you take as many pictures as you like in the Winter Wonderland, but please stay within the candy cane markers.

"Thank you all for coming and sharing your time with us! Show your hand stamp in Della department store today for fifteen percent off all your Della purchases." One last huge smile and wave—she hoped no one saw how she sweated.

As she retreated, Marcus—stationed near Santa's chair—caught up to her. "Is St. Nick here yet?"

"No."

"Then how's he going to be on stage in just a few minutes?"

"I didn't know what else to say. I'd put one of you guys in the Santa suit, but Bourbon Bob ruined it. The new guy is bringing his own suit."

"How long do we wait?"

Alyson stared at Marcus, hoping she didn't look as desperate as she felt. She had no Plan B. "I'm calling the agency again. I'll let you know."

"Seems I'm in the right place at the right time after all. I got this." He turned toward the crowd.

"Marcus, please." She touched his forearm—so warm to her icy fingers. His surprised gaze fell to where she had touched him. "Please don't go off script. Not yet. I'm trying to get promoted, not fired." Her eyes teared with frustration and feeling the tears only made her more frustrated. "Everything has to be perfect. I can't handle another disaster. Please."

"There's a lot of unhappy people out there."

His gentle voice surprised her. Whatever pleading he saw in her eyes had him caving.

"All right. I'll wait. But life doesn't follow a script." His voice held a warning.

She nodded, but he had already turned back to face the crowd.

Back in the workshop, she called the agency, left a message, and tried everything she could to get to a human instead of stuck in a machine loop. She called coworkers and her neighbor, anyone she knew who could possibly fill in, but none had a Santa suit, and the local costume shop was all out.

Now fifteen minutes behind schedule, she felt horrible for the poor elves—she knew the parents' patience was wearing thin.

Alyson came back out, climbed only a few of the steps, just enough to see and take the temperature of the crowd. Irritated, for sure. A family from the middle of the line went around the red ropes to leave, walking through the fake snow and ruining part of the Wonderland. Even her own sons and mom looked dour, hopeless. The first family who had arrived early had already been waiting at least forty-five minutes.

She covered her eyes with her hand. This was the absolute worst Christmas ever, and she was the one in charge. This was her failure. Worst of all, these children would walk away thinking Santa didn't care. Maybe this would be the year they stopped believing, all because she couldn't pull this together.

Her throat clogged with the shame of failure. She pressed her hand against her mouth, not allowing a single sob to escape, but tears rolled. She was the fixer, the problem solver. People depended on her.

All these families depended on them, on her, to make Christmas come alive for their little ones. Instead, she was merely reinforcing hopelessness, neglect, broken promises. It was her fault. All her fault her boys didn't have a Santa, didn't have a daddy this Christmas.

She closed her eyes against the tears. *Please, God. Please don't let it end this way. Don't let us end on misery.*

A clear, strong masculine voice singing "God Rest Ye Merry Gentlemen" rose above the angry hum of the crowd. Marcus was singing. Really well. And some of the crowd were joining in.

As the surprise song neared its end, people started shouting out Christmas carol titles. Marcus started on "We Three Kings." He hollered "Men, sing along," and she was surprised to hear many more male voices joining in, their strong voices filling the mall.

The voices of men, women, and children resonating through the halls gave her goosebumps and raised the weight from her shoulders. So joyful, it brought fresh tears to her eyes. She climbed the rest of the steps to the stage, wiping her eyes before coming into view. Then Marcus led all the children in "Rudolph, the Red-Nosed Reindeer," complete with hand motions. Did he have kids of his own? He was so good with them.

When Marcus noticed her, he held in his gaze the question they all had at the top of their minds. She shook her head. No Santa.

When the song ended, he turned to the crowd and asked the first twenty or so kids to come up on the stage, and he would tell a story. They did, including her boys, Darius waving at her slyly as if they shared a big secret with her real identity, and little Andre pointing at her wig and bonnet with a mistrustful frown.

If there would be no Santa, at least she could spend this time with her boys. She went to them and sat as best she could on the steps. Andre called out a happy "Mama!" as he realized it was really her, then climbed onto her lap, wrapping his chubby little arms around her neck, the best feeling in the world.

Darius started to tell her about the singing she'd missed, and she kissed his head and redirected his attention to Marcus for the story. "But Mom, it's Mr. Powell!" She cocked her head at her son, then looked at Marcus with a squint of recognition. Her Elfin Linebacker was Darius's music teacher?

Marcus met her gaze, and though she tried to say thank you with her eyes, he was apologizing with his. Why? He'd brought joy to a hopeless situation, one she'd failed to control. What did he have to be sorry for?

Once as many as could fit were settled on the steps before Santa's chair, Marcus recited a dramatic version of "'Twas the Night Before Christmas," complete with sound effects that made the children laugh. Then he seamlessly led into a story about who the real Saint Nickolas was, telling them of his legendary generosity. Marcus's soulful voice riveted children and parents alike. Riveted Alyson.

"So even when the rule-makers told him he must stop, he still made gifts of toys and food for the needy families. The authorities didn't like him because he disobeyed their rules, but he knew what was *right*. He knew what God had commanded him to do, and that was to take care of everyone he could in the way that he could. That was his gift from God and his purpose."

Marcus paused, looking at each child before him. "So when you finally do get to talk to Santa or your parents, or when you pray, ask for something for someone else, for your brother or sister or friend. Make a wish for someone who needs more than you do. And in that way, we can all have the spirit of Christmas inside us."

Alyson covered her mouth with her hand. She wished she could take back everything she'd ever said to him—she'd misjudged him again and again. Her throat burned with gratitude and newfound deep respect.

Beep-beep-beep! A loud, high-pitched horn in the hallway. She whipped her head around to locate the sound, her full heart suddenly in a panic, expecting the worst. *Beep-beep beeeeeeep!*

"Here comes Santa Claus!" A child yelled from the edge of the crowd. Alyson strained to see the direction the child was pointing. A thrill of excitement swept through the crowd as more and more people said, "I see him, I see him!" and "There he is!"

Santa, dressed in full regalia, rode in a security golf cart, coming as fast as the mall traffic would allow. He stood and waved, and the crowd roared and waved back, little kids jumping up and down. Even she was jumping up and down on the inside. Judging by the noise, you'd think a rock star was in the house.

Marcus started clapping and singing, "Here Comes Santa Claus," and the crowd joined in.

By the time Jolly old Saint Nick made it up the stage steps, he was winded, but he looked like the real deal, including the rosy cheeks and twinkling blue eyes. He waved to the crowd and said, "Sorry I'm late! I got called away and when I got back— well, do you know how hard it is to park a sleigh and eight reindeer? *Oy vey!*"

Chapter Two

Marcus took his position next to Santa and watched Alyson Stefanelli lead her boys and the other children and parents back to the line behind the velvet ropes.

She was smiling and acting the part of Mrs. Claus again, but her toddler had her wig in his grasp, trying to pull off the offending creature. Laughing, she handed the little boy to an older woman, who must be her mother, then righted the wronged wig.

Before today, he'd thought his beautiful, fashionista boss was just the usual vain type of women he'd met in college. He'd been drawn to her when they first met—had felt that rare zing when she shook his hand and looked in his eyes at the start of his interview—but he had resisted it, not wanting to repeat old mistakes and hard-learned lessons.

And yet, everything changed the moment he heard Darius call her Mom. She wasn't who she pretended to be.

"Bring on the good little boys and girls! Santa's ready!" The old man settled himself on the big red pillow he'd brought.

Smart man. Marcus saluted Santa and helped the first family.

As the young girl spoke to Santa in broken English, Marcus stole a peek at Darius and his little brother in line, each holding a hand of their grandma, a small porcelain-white woman with dark red hair. And now that he looked closely, she had the same fine-boned features as Alyson, only more delicate, almost birdlike. Same rosebud lips. Darius waved, catching his eye, reminding him not to stare. He waved back, with a smile for his favorite student.

Darius had been at the school less than three weeks when the school counselor pleaded with Marcus to work with the boy one-on-one after school because the state-sponsored program had kicked Darius out for his inability to play well with others. The third-grader was already branded a loner who picked fights and damaged property.

When the counselor told him about the sudden divorce and the family driving across country to live with the grandmother, Marcus couldn't refuse. It had taken weeks to get Darius to open up and stop acting out. Music had been the key.

It was hard to believe his uptight, snobby boss was Darius's mom. She was obviously using her maiden name again, at least at work. That's why he hadn't made the connection to Darius Daniels.

His heart fell at the thought of what she'd been through. Now it made sense why she kept her distance, froze people out. The motley group of elves went out for a beer or coffee after closing, but she always went back to work.

Before, he'd thought she just considered all of them beneath her. Now? It seemed she had her priorities straight. She worked hard then went home to her children. Did it hurt for her to see the others celebrate their easy freedom?

Darius had internalized such rage from the divorce. What had it done to her?

Santa signaled he was ready for the next family. Marcus guided a preteen girl and her mom along and ended up taking photos with the mom's phone while they both posed with Santa.

The next child was Darius, holding the hand of his little brother, who eyed Santa warily. Their grandmother followed behind a few steps, wearing a proud smile.

"Hey, Mr. Powell!" Darius grabbed his hand. "Can we sing like that at school?"

"It'll be January when we're back at school, Dare, but I'll teach you some other songs. You want to be in the school play?"

"Are you doing it? Or Miss Allen?"

"I'm doing the music. She's doing the play."

"I want to do the music too." Darius beamed up at him.

Marcus was used to the kids idolizing him, but it always pained his heart. He and the coach were the only male role models many of the kids had. He patted Darius toward Santa.

"I've got him, sir." Darius lifted his little brother onto Santa's lap then stood back, arms crossed, like a mini adult.

Their grandmother told Santa the boys' names.

"And what do you want for Christmas, Andre?"

"Want Mama back."

"You're okay, sweetie." His grandma rubbed his arm. "Just tell Santa what toys you want."

"No"—Darius shook his head—"he wants Mom home more. She's always working."

"Darius, honey." She shook her head quickly and glanced at Marcus with a small, tight smile. "Your mom needs to work."

Marcus got the idea it embarrassed her to discuss such things in front of strangers. "We all work, little man." Marcus tipped his red and green pointed hat, making Darius smile.

"What about you, Darius?" Santa studied him over his wire-rimmed spectacles. "What can Santa bring *you* for Christmas?"

Marcus knew why the man had phrased it that way, to get him to focus on toys or games, but

Darius's thoughtful silence had him afraid the poor kid was going to wish for his dad to come back or some other heart-wrenching, impossible task.

"I don't know." He shrugged. "A football, I guess. I just want Mom to be happy again." Darius nodded. "Yeah. Everything was great back when Mom was happy."

ᔥᔣ

"Yo, Marcus," Bert leaned up against the wall of cubbies that acted as a makeshift locker room. "You coming tonight? We're headed to that new club, *Tight*. Wanna go?"

Marcus looked him over. Bert had already changed into all black, including a silk tie, with his hair slicked back.

"Naw, y'all go on without me. You clean up too good, Bert, I wouldn't have a chance. Just your wingman."

"Bro. Whatever. I'll get more chicks without you there, but it'll be more fun *with* you." He held his hands out, one last plea.

"Have fun, yo."

Bertie smacked his shoulder. "Next time."

Marcus gave him a single nod. As soon as Bert left the room, Marcus stopped pretending he was busy and sat on the bench, wondering if the words he needed would ever come to him in time or if he would leave without talking to Alyson.

He heard a thud in the main room and knew she must have arrived. He rounded the cubbies. Alyson had her back to him and had set a banker's box on the folding table that acted as her desk.

He watched her stretch high with a yawn, then pull on the back of her neck like she needed a massage. She bent down and unbuckled her shoes and rubbed her arches, her skirt tight across her backside.

Although he loved the view, he felt like a perv watching her and cleared his throat to announce himself as he walked farther into the main room. "Hey."

Alyson spun around, eyes wide. "Oh! I'm so sorry. I thought everyone had gone." Her cheeks and the tips of her ears bloomed pink. She started to put her heels back on.

"Hey, no need for that. Keep 'em off. Relax a little."

She hesitated, but slipped them back on anyway. As he stepped closer, she moved behind the desk. She took the lid off the box, pretending to continue working, but her body was stiff. Why was she nervous? She seemed as nervous as he felt.

"I'm glad you're still here," she said. "I wanted to thank you for . . . for saving the show. You were wonderful. I had given up, and you . . ."

When she met his gaze he felt like it was the first time she was truly seeing him.

"It was beautiful what you did, Marcus. You really made the day special for all those families. Something they'll never forget." She pressed her lips together and looked away, down.

Why was she suddenly sad?

He wanted to take away the hurt. But he didn't know what to say. He never knew what to say.

"Anyway." She shook her head and didn't look up. "Thank you for being my hero today."

He chuckled. Hero. For singing a few songs. But he still liked hearing it. "Hey, I wear tights. That's *superhero* attire."

She smiled brightly, eyes twinkling with humor. "Yeah, you've got the look for that. Superhero, then."

How did a woman this beautiful not get everything she wanted out of life? How could anyone refuse such a smile? "I think I owe you an apology."

"Why? What for?"

"Assuming you had something against me because I'm black and tatted up."

Her face fell. "Marcus, I'm so sorry if I offended you." She touched his arm in apology, her huge dark eyes pleading. "Honestly, I'm in such a rush I don't even hear what I'm saying half the time. If I hurt you, please forgive me."

Her fingers felt cool on his arm, and when she pulled away and clasped her hands, a nervous little smile playing at her lips, all Marcus could feel was the absence of her touch. The spot felt suddenly empty. He resisted the urge to cover it with his other hand. "Hey, now. I was trying to apologize to you. You're stealing my apology."

She smiled again, genuinely, showing dimples he hadn't realized she had. "I'll accept yours if you accept mine."

He returned the smile.

She held his gaze only a moment before her smile dropped, her eyes wide with alarm, like she'd just remembered she left the oven on or a candle lit.

She bowed her head. "Goodnight, Marcus. Have fun at that new club everyone's raving about." She pulled the open box toward her, a faint, polite smile once again on her lips. The 'perfect' smile she used with customers and mall patrons.

He took a half-step back, trying to figure out what had turned her off so fast. They were finally being real with each other and she does the turtle, pulling her head into her shell. Why?

"Naw, I'm not dressed for it. And if you can't wear jeans and sneaks, I'm not going." Truthfully, he hated the synthesized beats and people at their nastiest. He tapped the box. "What's all this?"

"Applications for more elves, paperwork for shoplifters, and two registers aren't balancing." She pulled on the back of her neck again. "But at least I found someone to cover your hours tomorrow and fixed some redundancies. So that's taken care of."

It bothered him that she never lifted her gaze from the box, wouldn't meet his eye anymore. "So . . . what? You're going to work all night?"

"Not here. I'll take it home. I came to get my other shoes."

His jaw dropped. "No way! Those mystery shoes are yours?" He took the few strides to fetch them from the cubbies. They were the ugliest, scruffiest running shoes he had ever seen. The tread had worn off. What had once been white was a weird gray-yellow. No one had claimed them, so they had figured they were left over from Bad Santa. "No. Seriously, girl. Just . . . no."

She laughed. "I can't throw them away. They're too comfortable."

"Why do you kill yourself wearing those sexy heels if this is what you really want?" He set them on the box top.

She stared at him in surprise like what he'd said meant more than he thought.

"I should get going." She didn't move, though, staring at him as if waiting for him to say something.

He motioned toward the door with an open palm. "Okay. No one's stopping you."

"Right." She took the sneakers and threw them into the box.

Her face reddened like she was embarrassed. For what? What did he say? And was she really so uptight she wouldn't even change her shoes in front of him?

She set the box on her hip and walked toward the door, jangling her keys.

He followed. "I'll walk you to your car."

She opened the door and waited for him to go out. "No. I'll be fine on my own." She struggled to hold the box as she tried to lock the door.

He wondered at the sudden testiness of her voice and took the box from her before she dropped it. "Doesn't mean you have to *do* everything alone. You know, Bertie and I keep offering to do more."

"I know. I'm sorry." Pulling and lifting the wobbly door with one hand, she easily turned the key with the other. "I should have involved you two in the planning. We'll work out your new positions on Monday. You're obviously the entertainer. I get it now." She tried to take the box from him. "I walk alone in the parking garage all the time. It's perfectly safe."

He didn't let go. "You need to let people help you."

Hands on hips, she narrowed her eyes at him. "I didn't ask for your opinion."

"Can't stop me from having one." He nodded toward the department store. "You park in that lot, right? Lead on."

She rolled her eyes at the chivalry but started toward the garage without further fight. "Fine."

They didn't say a word to each other as they walked through the closing mall, the only sounds the lonesome metronome of her heels, the rhythmic hum of the large machine floor waxers and the occasional far-off walkie-talkie sounding as the cleaning crews reported in.

When they reached the top level of the garage, open to the chilly December breeze, Marcus was surprised to see so many cars. It seemed every department store in the mall must have employees still working well past closing.

He was even more surprised to see Alyson stop at a red Mercedes SUV and open the back door, bending to move things around so he could set the box inside. He purposefully shifted his gaze away from her backside. His eye caught a sign in the back window that said "For Sale—Serious Offers Only" and a phone number.

"How much you asking?" He set the box on the back seat next to a car seat and a snack bag of Cheerios.

"What? Oh, for the car? Just the blue book value. I don't really want to sell it, but it makes no practical sense to keep it." She frowned, sticking out her bottom lip in an exaggerated pout. "I love my car."

"It's practical if it's paid off. Or is that why you're working so much overtime?"

She smiled and shook her head. "No, it's paid off. But I could buy three used cars for the price of this baby. And it costs a lot to maintain. I have to think of the future. It needs to go." She caressed the leather seat back like it was the arm of a dying loved one.

"One of the last vestiges of another life. Like my pretty shoes." She tapped her toes together. "I'd had this pair in my closet for a couple years and never wore them." Her face darkened. "By the way, I'm selling all my designer clothes, shoes, bags, even perfumes if you know anyone who'd be interested. Good prices." She sighed. "All used goods."

She shut the back door, hard. A frown settled on her pretty mouth.

Marcus got the idea they weren't talking about her shoes anymore. "Hey, you want to get coffee? I know a great little diner near here."

"Don't try to be nice to me, Marcus. I know what you're doing, and I don't accept your pity. I'm a big girl, and yes, I *can* do this on my own. I have to." She got into the driver's seat but hesitated before closing the door. "Do you need a ride to your car?"

"No, I walk."

"Walk?"

He laughed at how surprised she was. "Yeah, you know, with legs. I only live about a mile away."

"Oh. You live near the elementary school?"

"Yeah, moved close to work."

"Well, shoot, you're a neighbor. Get in. I'll take you home."

"Naw. That's all right. I like the walk."

"You worked a double. I know you've got to be tired. Come on. Hop in."

"No. I can do this on *my own*." Marcus adopted a falsetto and put his hand on his hip. "I don't *need* any friends."

Her head cocked, her mouth hung open.

Bingo.

She slammed the door.

Marcus started toward the stairs as the Mercedes roared to life but stopped to wave as the SUV retreated around the tight corner of the garage. The words he'd used were not exactly *smooth* but had been effective. He had to trust getting under her skin was the best way to get her attention. Deep inside, he felt that God had put her in his path for a reason, he felt that deep inside. At the moment, he just wasn't sure why.

Chapter Three

Marcus, full-bellied and warm in the diner, kept his face buried in his book, suffering along with Frodo and Sam on their long trek to Mordor. He grabbed his iced water and slurped. He abandoned the hobbits, setting his open book down on the table while he craned his neck looking for the waitress.

Out of the corner of his eye, he saw a shiny red Mercedes pull up outside. A little zing ran down his neck and shoulders. He watched as Alyson got out of her SUV and opened the back door to retrieve the box he'd put in there about an hour ago. *What are you up to, God? What did you want me to do that I didn't do?* He knew God would keep putting her in his path until he did the right thing, whatever that was.

She slammed it shut with her hip, carrying the banker's box inside the diner. She wore yoga pants and a fitted hoodie, her hair piled on her head in a messy bun. No makeup. He might be seeing the real Alyson for a change.

She came in and bypassed a ten-top of noisy older folks celebrating. With her head down, she walked into the quieter section he was in and slid the box into the next booth and sat. He put a smile on his face, thinking she was about to look up any second and see him, but the waitress came to her table, taking her attention.

"*Mija*! Where have you been, *mija*? Your *mami* came in with the boys today after they saw Santa. We missed you." She set a coffee and creamers on the table. "Your usual, *mija*?"

"No, Luisa, I'm going to be horribly, deliciously, wantonly bad tonight and have a cinnamon roll. *With extra butter*." The last said in a villainous tone.

His smile spread.

"Ohhh. I'll warm it up for you just right so the butter gets all melty."

"You get me, Luisa."

The waitress smiled and patted Alyson's shoulder. As Alyson turned back to her papers her gaze slid over him, and she did a double take. Her smile turned to a frown.

"You want more water, sir?" Luisa zoomed over and grabbed his glass before he had a chance to answer.

"Yes, thank you." But she was already on her way to the drink station with his glass.

He shifted his gaze back to Alyson, not entirely surprised to see her glower.

"What are you doing here?" Eyes narrowed, her voice a harsh whisper. "Are you stalking me?"

"Hey, I was here first." He waved at his empty plate with a chuckle.

"I've been coming here since I was *born*. This is *my* diner."

The waitress set his iced water before him and looked from him to Alyson and back again. "Is something wrong, Alyson?"

"Everything's fine. Really. He's a colleague."

"Well, you let me know if I have to get someone, okay?" She whispered and glanced suspiciously at him as she walked back to the kitchen.

He rolled his eyes. No matter where he was or what he was doing, he always faced the stigma of being a large black man. But he saved his disappointment for Alyson. "Colleague?" He shook his head. "You couldn't have said 'He's a *friend* of mine'?"

"I'm sorry. I didn't expect my worlds to collide like that."

"You know what, *Ms. Stefanelli*? It's all cool. I'm minding my own business reading my book. You do your thing. Just two strangers." He picked up his book.

"Fine with me."

He read the same sentences over and over as he listened to her unpack the box and organize her workspace.

Hearing the clicking of nails on keys, he looked up and saw she was comparing a computer printout with a cash register receipt roll and punching in data on a clunky beige adding machine that looked like it had been brand new back in the 1980s.

He refocused his attention on his book and ignored her. Mostly.

Luisa brought her cinnamon roll and refreshed her coffee. The table of seniors erupted in a volley of greetings as four more people joined the group. Luisa didn't stick around this time, heading instead for the newcomers.

Alyson looked over her shoulder at the revelers, then back at the papers and cinnamon roll. Her shoulders slumped, and she started to pack up.

"Hey, you better eat that while it's warm." He coveted that gooey sugar bomb.

"I can't concentrate." She thumbed over her shoulder at the large group just as one of the men belly laughed, and the others followed suit.

"You want my headphones?" He pulled them from his backpack. "I'm not using them." He took the two steps to hand the full-coverage headphones to her. "Why'd you come here to concentrate? Isn't it quieter at home?"

She had to tilt her head back to meet his gaze, so he sat down across from her. She held the headphones as if weighing them, but he could tell by the faraway look in her eyes she was weighing something else in her mind, as though accepting the headphones carried a deeper meaning. Or maybe she still didn't trust him.

"Well. I guess you've gathered I live with my mom, right?"

"Yeah. Lots of people move back home. Nothing wrong with that."

"We've never gotten along. I was Daddy's girl, and my sister was always Mom's favorite. Mom was getting ready to sell the house and retire to California to be with my sister's family, and I kind of ruined that. She's leaving tomorrow to spend Christmas with them." She took a huge bite of the cinnamon roll, but she didn't seem to get any joy from it, the frown still there.

"We fight," she said, still chewing. "A lot. She nags me about all the bad decisions I've made. As if I didn't know. I mean, I'm the one living the result, right?"

Another bite and more gesticulating with the fork. He seemed to have gone from stalker to girlfriend in nothing flat. Why had she let her guard down?

He stopped himself from smiling at how much she talked with her hands when she wasn't at work—she was like two different people. Work-

Alyson was sexy and cold. But this one? Real. He'd take this Alyson over the other one in a heartbeat.

"So, long story not much shorter, I can't get anything done there. I hear her disapproval even when she's asleep. It hangs in the air." She waggled the fingers of one hand in front of her face and shoved another bite of sugar therapy into her mouth with the other.

"All moms do that. I can't go home without getting an earful." It was a slight exaggeration. The earful he usually got was about how he didn't visit often enough. But Alyson needed sympathy, not comparison.

"Where's home?" She covered her cinnamon-roll-stuffed mouth with her fingertips this time. Eyes inquisitive, not just being polite.

"Houston."

"Nice. Close enough to visit, but far enough away for the distance to be a good excuse *not* to visit." She cut another bite with her fork and stopped. "You want some? You'd be doing me a favor. I don't need all these calories."

"Naw, I don't eat that stuff anymore."

"I know I shouldn't give in to emotional eating, but I don't care. Stop judging me."

"Not judging."

"Luisa?" She craned her neck, half-turning in her seat to talk to the woman. "Another fork, please."

Long, graceful neck, delicate collar bone he could trace with a fingertip. With effort, he brought his gaze to the table.

She was still his boss for two more days. The others would see it on him in a second if he didn't get control of this stupid . . . whatever it was. He was too old to be crushing on someone. And it definitely didn't fit his plans.

He caught himself—*This isn't about me. It's about her and Darius. And little Andre. Don't be a jerk.*

Luisa delivered another fork and a large glass of milk, "Here you go, *mija*. To help you sleep. It's not too hot?"

"It's perfect. Thank you." Alyson took a big drink of the milk and smiled at the waitress.

Luisa delivered his bill to him where he sat. "Anything else for you tonight, sir?"

He marveled at how she could be so motherly toward Alyson and then so professional toward him. "No, thanks. How long have you known Alyson that she gets the princess treatment?"

"Oh, her whole life! *Mi princesa*. I am her godmother." The woman touched her heart proudly. "This is her home away from home. She used to run away and come here to me." She drew out the last word with a smile. "It was the cutest thing. All of ten years old and crying and carrying on like she was going to hop a train and become a hobo."

Alyson hid her face behind her hand and shook her head, but her huge smile and pinking cheeks encouraged Luisa.

"Then her *papi* would come to get her after a while and they'd sit and have pie and talk it over. Real serious like. Like working through her plan, you know? Always leave the decision up to her. So cute. *Mija*, you were so cute." Luisa gave her a sideways hug. "I miss your *papi*. He was a good man."

Alyson patted her hand, still on her shoulder. "I miss him too."

He saw no sadness in Alyson's sympathetic smile, only love. But something inside was broken or she wouldn't have closed herself off from everyone at work, refusing friendship, even the smallest kindness as if she didn't deserve it. She wouldn't have to be two different people if everything was okay inside.

The bell from the kitchen dinged and Luisa left to pick up the order.

Alyson snatched his ticket from his hand.

"I knew it! Grilled chicken salad. And here I am stuffing my face full of fat and sugar."

"No need to compare." He grabbed it back. It wasn't exactly the manliest thing on the menu, but he wouldn't allow himself to eat anything other than a salad this late at night. He didn't want to undo all his hard work.

"Well, that's why you're in such good shape and my clothes are getting too tight."

"Just right from where I'm sitting."

He expected a raised brow or a smirk like most girls, but she looked dumbfounded, like even the mildest flirting was a shock to the system.

He tapped the adding machine to change the topic. "Why are you working doubles all the time? And then unpaid overtime like this?"

"Do I have to state the obvious?"

He was glad she didn't stay focused on his appreciation of her curves. He'd better cool it and start thinking before he spoke. "Yeah, yeah, we all need money, but what exactly do you need the money for? I mean, you're living with your mom, right? So you don't have that many bills . . ."

"I'll need my own place soon. And tuition. Someday. I need to finish my degree if I'm ever going to make store management." She wrinkled her nose like something smelled bad.

He chuckled at the beautiful princess making faces. "I take it that's not what you want?"

She shrugged.

"Then why's it your goal?"

"I only have one more year of classes to finish my business administration degree. I can't afford to start over."

"What would you do if money wasn't an issue?"

"What would *you* do?" She leaned back, hitching one arm on the back of the booth. It opened her zip-up hoodie more, giving a better view of her chest in a neon green exercise tank.

He breathed out with puffed cheeks and picked up the extra fork to dig into the cinnamon roll. New reason for stress eating. He kept his eyes off of her. *You aren't making this easy for me, are you, God? Sure, help the beautiful woman I can't take my eyes off of. Thanks for nothing.*

"Believe it or not, I'm doing what I want to do. For now, anyway. Money could be better, but it's enough for a single guy." He took the bite of cinnamon roll and regretted it. Too sweet, cloying. He put the fork down and leaned back. "I've got summers off to tour with my band. I do A/V work for my church. You should come sometime." He studied her to gauge her reaction.

"What instrument do you play?"

Even though he'd set her up for it, she'd avoided asking him where he went to church. Very telling. She probably did not attend. And by asking a question, she definitely wanted to keep the conversation away from herself.

He wasn't about to let her off that easy. "No, no. I answered the question. Now you have to. What would *you* do if money wasn't an issue?"

"Law school. I helped put my ex through law school, and I helped him study. I even researched for him when he had a case. I was practically his paralegal and his secretary, early on. I know I can do it because I already have, just not for me."

"What happened? Sounds like you had a great partnership."

He realized his mistake only after he'd said it. Of course they didn't have a great partnership if it ended in divorce. Especially if the divorce was as sudden as Darius had talked about. Marcus wondered what could have happened, but knew they weren't close enough yet to pry. And thanks to his big mouth she had shut down, lips tense, face blank, hard.

"Lawyer, huh? I can see that. Criminal law?"

"Family law. I want to be the kind of lawyer I wish I'd had. Someone has to advocate for the people who are hurting too much to think clearly. I know I made some stupid mistakes. I knew better, but I . . . I just wanted it to be over."

"Maybe that's why it all happened. Maybe God's pushing you to be that lawyer who helps families. Give you the motivation."

She leveled her gaze at him, and he knew instantly he had said the wrong thing. Again.

"Thanks. That's just what I need to hear. God destroyed our lives for someone else's alleged future convenience. Very helpful." She downed the rest of her coffee. "Besides, if He's providing motivation, then He can certainly provide the means, too, and I haven't seen that coming my way." She shook her head, looking into the empty coffee cup. "Law school is too expensive. I can't even afford daycare. I certainly can't do both."

The silence grew. The laughter from the table of older folks stood out in stark contrast to the glum atmosphere surrounding them. He hadn't meant to bring her down. He wasn't helping at all. But at least he'd gleaned that she was probably a Christian . . . or once was. How could he help her mend that most important relationship?

Another car pulled up right outside their window, drawing his attention. The couple looked at the "For Sale" sign in the window of Alyson's Mercedes before walking to the diner's entrance.

That's it. That's how I can help.

"Hey, I can sell that 'cedes for you. My uncle's a car dealer in Houston. He'll give you a fair price."

She wasn't saying no, even seemed to be thinking it over.

"Especially if you buy a used car too. Want me to contact him?"

"No. That's okay." The little worry line settled between her brows. "I don't know when I'd have the time to get to Houston, anyway."

He wanted to take his thumb and rub that little worry line away. "Now, now. Don't shoot it down completely. Let's take pics and send them to Uncle Mason and see what he says before you decide, okay?"

He didn't wait for her answer this time but instead grabbed his phone and went outside to take some photos. He sent them with a text with a simple message: "Friend of mine." It was late, but he knew if his uncle was still awake and interested he'd phone immediately. It was just a few seconds before he felt the phone vibrate. *Yes!*

Uncle Mason wasted no time with small talk. "Asking price?"

"Blue book value. And she needs a cheap replacement. But good and safe. She has two kids. One is my favorite student. And she's good people, needs decent money for her car. Did I mention the two kids? Young ones."

"What's wrong with it?"

"Nothing. Great condition." His uncle was a sucker for a hard luck story. He had to punch this up a notch. "Got it in a rough divorce and wants to be free of it, and she needs the money really bad for daycare. Single mom. All alone. She's totally going to be taken advantage of if you don't help her out, Uncle Mason. Can you get a buyer for her?"

He could tell by the short silence and soft grumbling he'd won his uncle over but that he wasn't happy about it.

"If the interior is good—"

"It is. I've seen it." Barely, but all he'd seen amiss was Cheerio crumbs, and those could be vacuumed in a flash.

"I may have a buyer already if he'll accept red instead of black."

"That's great!"

"You realize I'm not making any money from this, right?"

"But she'll get that Toyota off your lot, finally."

"And what are you going to drive? I thought you wanted that Toyota."

"We can discuss that when I get there. I've got to fit in the driver's seat, you know."

"I make no promises, Marcus. Ask her to send me proof of maintenance, the VIN and mileage."

"Thanks, Uncle May! We'll see you on Christmas!" He hung up before his uncle could respond.

He glided back in and fell into the booth, sitting back against the wall, his legs outstretched along the seat. "Okay, so my uncle has this Toyota that isn't sexy enough to move off his lot. He mostly sells used luxury and sports cars. You'd be doing him a favor if you buy that Toyota, and he'll find a buyer for your Mercedes." He relayed the details of what Mason wanted from her.

"Oh, that's no problem. I've already scanned all of that with my private info redacted. It's in the cloud, so we can send that right now and text the mileage."

"He's going to love you. He sees you're that organized he'll trust this is a good vehicle for his buyer."

"But how do I get the car to him?"

"You have vacation time saved up?"

"I can't—"

"No. No. Hear me out. We drive to Houston on Christmas Eve after you get off work. Christmas is an all-day party. Day after, we make the deal with Uncle Mason, then you can drive away whenever you feel like. Or stay one more day and come to church with us.

"The Sunday after Christmas is always super relaxed and filled with music. You'd love it. It's like having another Christmas party but with the whole congregation. Your boys would love it. Lots of kids there. Dad always makes me do something embarrassing, so you can get a good laugh if you stay the extra day."

"What do you mean?"

"Preacher's kid." He saw the dawning realization on her face. "Don't judge me. I see that look on your face. Don't act like you know who I am."

She smiled wide and bright. "I won't, I promise. As long as you do the same for me."

"Deal."

They shook on it. The moment took on weight as they continued to smile at each other, as though their friendship had just begun. He let go of her hand, realizing he'd held it too long. "Can you get that time off?"

That worry line was back. "Are there gifts at this party? I don't think we should be there for the gifts, Marcus. I can't afford—"

"Nonsense. I'm the youngest of five. I have fourteen nieces and nephews. Mom has a closet full of toys and stuff 'just in case' because she loves being a grandma to absolutely everybody. Your boys will have a blast. No doubt about it."

"I . . . I don't know. I mean, it sounds wonderful . . . and thank you, but . . ."

"One, don't worry about the whole supervisor-employee thing because that's all over in a few days anyway, right? Two, you need this money. Three, you'll actually get a break, and get some great food because my mom is the best cook in the world. And four, if you don't come with me because of some work obligation, good luck on finding an all-day babysitter the day after Christmas."

She cast her gaze downward and puckered her lips like she was mulling it over.

"And five, you haven't had a full day off in how many days? Isn't that illegal?"

"No, you're right. Mr. Giles promised me time off after Christmas if I took over the Winter Wonderland. And you have no idea how much I hate doing returns. The week after Christmas is horrible." She picked up her fork again and scooped up some icing from the plate. "And Darius can be such a handful when he gets bored. It would be great to be around other kids, so he could play."

"Then it's settled. You're coming home with me." Tingles in his gut signaled this was important. But maybe he shouldn't have said it like that. She wasn't smiling.

A confusing mix of emotions rolled over her face—gratitude warring with distrust.

"Why are you helping me? Why are you even being nice to me? What's in it for you?"

"What? It's Christmas." He shrugged. It sounded weak. He wouldn't believe it either, but he couldn't tell her he felt God had put them in each other's paths for a purpose—she'd think he was a religious zealot and run away.

Nor could he tell her about the stupid crush strengthening every time he saw little glimpses of who she really was behind her mask of polished efficiency.

He wasn't sure why he had to help her. He just knew he had to. It *felt* right. "Well, you'll be giving me a ride to Houston. See? It's a win-win."

Her one raised eyebrow said she didn't believe him, but she didn't press the issue further.

Marcus smiled. Introducing unknowns into the mix would be like a chemical reaction in the family—anything could happen. This wasn't going to be the same old holiday.

Chapter Four

Alyson wiped the remains of Andre's messy eating from the dinner table while her mom set the pots and pans in the sink. "Are you going to be okay with that guy?"

Alyson dumped a handful of rice and peas into the garbage. "Yes, Mom, I trust him, and Darius loves him. You've heard him talk about Mr. Powell this and Mr. Powell that."

"And you two have become fast friends. Why all of a sudden?"

Alyson thought a moment against the backdrop of her mom filling the sink with soapy water, raising suds. "He's the only one who cares enough to try. He doesn't let me hide."

Her mom turned off the water. "What was that, honey? Couldn't hear you. The sprayer was on."

"Nothing." Alyson didn't dare say it twice. "We'll be fine, Mom." It was almost time to leave for the airport. Her mom had packed light, but Alyson had the feeling she wouldn't be coming back any time soon. It was a one-way ticket, after all. She'd only return to finalize the sale of the house, whenever that happened.

"Sweetheart." Her mom came to her and gave her a hug. "I understand loneliness. I miss your father every single day. But you need to guard your heart a little. Don't fall for someone just because he's nice to you. You deserve more than that."

Alyson sank into her mother's arms. Finally, her mom understood.

"You can't afford to make the same mistake twice."

Alyson pulled out of the hug and bit back the sharp retort that came to mind. No sense in fighting in their last hour together.

"Way ahead of you on guarding my heart, Mom." Alyson picked up the keys. "Got your boarding pass?"

At work the next couple of days, everything seemed rosier. Videos of Marcus entertaining the crowd went viral and Della's sales had increased as the number of views increased. Mr. Giles came out to thank the crowds and took selfies with Marcus in his elf costume. People came to hear him as much as they came to see Santa.

But Alyson, sitting behind her makeshift desk in the workshop, was a nervous wreck. Already packed for their trip and ready to go, she couldn't shake the feeling that this was a huge mistake.

Colossal. It would fall apart, and she'd make a fool of herself. Her little family would be at the mercy of someone she hardly knew.

Marcus's whole family would see her as someone looking for a handout. She didn't have money for presents for them, and she couldn't go to someone's home and not bring a gift.

Glancing around the room, she wished it would clear of people faster so she could talk to Marcus alone. He'd also seemed a little out of sorts this afternoon as it got closer to time to leave. Had he changed his mind?

Bertie shot into the room, seemingly the only one with plenty of energy left. "You're a hit, brother!" He playfully punched Marcus in the arm. "You need to use all this newfound fame to market your band."

"We don't tour until summer, and we don't sing Christmas songs. This stupid elf costume is destroying my image. It's the first blasted thing that comes up online."

"Come on, man. Any publicity is good publicity."

Alyson watched the exchange with growing dread. Helping her had hurt Marcus. The resentment in his voice had her thinking of canceling the trip to Houston—she was a burden. But she was also his ride and couldn't change her mind now, not when he'd taken extra hours to match her schedule. She doubted he could get a bus to Houston this late.

She handed out the last checks to the temporary workers, who were excited to get out and go spend their pay.

As Marcus took his he said, "I've got a few last-minute things to get. I won't be long."

"Take your time. I've got to turn in this paperwork, and then I have to get the kids from the sitters. And we're all packed, including jackets for that cold front that's coming."

"Packed?" Bertie joined them at the table. "Where're you going? Some fancy ski lodge?"

She looked at Marcus, not knowing how to answer.

Marcus met her gaze and shrugged. "It's not like you're the boss lady anymore." He waved his final check in the air.

Bertie sat on the table and leaned in looking between them. "What is this? What. Is. This? Have y'all been sneaking behind our backs?"

"No!" Alyson took a step back from both of them.

"No, Bert, it's not like that." Then to her, "When should I come over?"

"All this time! Ohhh Emmm Geee, you guys!"

"You're not making this any better." She scowled at Marcus.

Marcus leaned in. "Does it really matter what they think?"

The low timbre of his voice . . . like a caress. *Ignore it. It's not for you.* "No, you're right." She would probably never see these people again anyway.

"Besides, would it be so horrible?" Marcus stood straight. "I'm not a stinky ogre or anything. Long car ride, though." He raised his arm and sniffed.

She rolled her eyes and shook her head, unable to stop her smile.

He matched it.

"I don't believe this," Bertie said. "Where are y'all going? Come on, I need deets."

Marcus's smile turned smug as if he liked having people wonder about their newfound friendship.

"Come on, Bertie, I need some fuel in me." He patted his flat stomach.

The action had her cheeks warming, and she looked away, pretending to be busier than she was. *Ignore. Ignore. Ignore.*

"Can I go?" Devon stepped in next to Bertie. The three walked out together, leaving her alone in the room. It seemed truly empty for the first time. Cold.

As much as she'd put into the Winter Wonderland the last few weeks, it was disappointing to see it go, to see how happy everyone was to go on their merry way. Leaving her alone. She wished she could be one of them, like Devon, young, carefree and up for whatever adventure. She wanted to go too. But duty called.

Suddenly all her worry about going to Houston with Marcus fell away. If she didn't go, what on earth would she do with herself over Christmas and her vacation time except beat herself up for all the wrong turns she'd made? Marcus was right. She needed a break, a rest, a fresh perspective, even if the thought of being a charity case made her skin crawl.

Chapter Five

Marcus turned onto Alyson's street, enjoying a walk in the approaching dusk, and spied the red Mercedes SUV from a distance. Most of the vehicles in the neighborhood were minivans and pickups. Ironic that a white flight neighborhood of the 1960s had become a well-mixed, working-class neighborhood. The change in demographics hadn't adversely affected the area one bit—it sported rising home values and some of the best schools in the city. He'd miss this humble, hard-working neighborhood when he moved to Hollywood.

He'd waited a full year for a house to come open, and when it did he'd pounced on it. When he told his family, instead of being happy for him they'd said, "If you've given up on Hollywood, why didn't you come home?" They couldn't understand his vision, his goals. He hadn't given up. He was just waiting for the right time.

As he rounded the SUV on the way to the front door, he paused, taking in the surprise of so much color in the careful, multi-level landscaping. So many shades of green, purple, white and red. With all these winter blooms, Alyson's mom definitely had a green thumb.

He knocked on the door and heard Darius scream, "I'll get it!" A moment later, Darius opened the door. Face beaming. "Yay! You're coming with us!"

He gave him a high five but corrected him with a smile. "You got it backward, little man. Y'all are coming with me. You're going to meet my mama."

Darius laughed as if his teacher having a mother was the most ridiculous thing in the world. He led Marcus into the house.

The first room was a library, all available wall space covered in adjustable shelves, layered in books. He wanted to take a closer look, but Darius ran ahead. "Mom! Mom! Mom! My Mr. Powell is here!"

"Thank you, Darius. Go change your shirt now, please, we're about to leave."

"Yes, ma'am!" Darius bolted to his room.

"Hi, Marcus. You really didn't have to walk over, we're only a couple minutes behind schedule." She looked at her watch. "No, I still have three minutes. Not that I would've been there in three minutes, but I would have called you." She didn't look up but continued taking pink cookies off a cookie sheet, placing them decoratively on a plastic tray. She was still dressed from work in skirt and heels, wearing an apron like a total 1950s throwback.

"No trouble. I got bored. What are those?"

"Cherry almond cookies. I made the shortbread last night. They're Christmas staples in my family. I hope they're acceptable."

"You don't have to bring anything."

"Of course I do, it's proper decorum."

"What era are you from? Who says that? *Proper decorum*. Trust me, there are so many sweets in that house you can get diabetes just walking in the door. You don't have to bring anything."

"Well, then . . . should I leave them here? Will your mom be *offended* if I bring something?"

Why was his usually confident boss—former boss—acting so unsure of herself? "No. Bring it. It'll be good to have something new."

He looked around while she finished up in the kitchen. The real reason he'd arrived unannounced—he wanted to check out her place and see what kind of woman he was dealing with. The house was spotless, all the wood furniture polished to a shine. But there was almost no decoration. Not even a Christmas tree, though there was still a bow and some torn paper on the floor near the fireplace.

Andre stood by the coffee table and continued building a tower out of huge interlocking blocks, totally uninterested in the fact they had a visitor. A red and green plaid stocking lay forgotten on the rug, chocolates and peppermint sticks, small cars, big rubber balls, and crayons spilled out from it in an arc.

A toy helicopter with remote control sat on the couch waiting to be played with. The other gift on the couch was a new car seat for Andre. Must be Alyson's gift from her mom. So, nothing for Alyson.

"I'll just be a minute more, I swear. The car is mostly loaded." She tore off a piece of plastic wrap and covered the tray of cookies. "Darius," she hollered. "You better not be destroying your clothes!" Then more softly to him with a shy smile, "He likes to unfold his clothes and put them on the floor where he can see them. Drives me nuts."

"I'm coming," Darius hollered back.

Marcus headed toward Darius's voice to stop him from destroying his room if that's what he was doing. But Darius met him in the hallway with a see-through plastic picnic basket of activity books and DVDs.

"Were you looking at my grandma?"

The question took him by surprise, but Darius nodded toward the framed photos on the wall. One a wedding portrait of Alyson's mom—extremely Irish-looking with her pale skin, red hair and blue eyes. And her dad—black wavy hair, deep olive skin and dark, penetrating eyes. Alyson seemed to be a good mix of her parents—her mother's hair and skin, but her father's eyes and jaw.

Another photo of two young girls dressed in matching outfits, their arms around each other like they were the best of friends. Twins. Dual cheerleading pics, dual prom pics. A family picture of the four of them, her father's hair still black, but his mustache and eyebrows coming in mostly white, both girls wearing white dresses like little brides, complete with lace veils covering their hair.

Then a photo of just the girls, each wearing a university sweatshirt—UCLA and UNC—from best of friends to opposite coasts.

"That's my aunt, Amy. I haven't seen her since I was little like Andre. Grandma went to see the new baby."

Though the sisters were identical, in each photo he could tell which one was Alyson by the intensity of her eyes. Extreme focus, driven. Even the girlish smile in the prom picture didn't hide her need to conquer. Her twin, Amy, looked somehow forgettable in comparison, though both were beauties.

"You ready?" Alyson was beside him suddenly, apron gone.

"Yeah, sure." Electricity shot through him like he'd been caught doing something wrong. Snooping.

"These are probably the only personal effects still in the house. Mom got rid of everything or put it in storage when she staged the house for the opening. But she didn't have the heart to take these down." She kissed her finger and touched it to her father's picture. "She said she wanted to prove that the house was filled with happiness once."

She looked at the picture a moment longer, then turned toward the front door and beckoned for him to follow. "My poor mom. I don't blame her at all for wanting to move away to California."

"Is that why there's no tree?"

"No. Mom hasn't celebrated Christmas since Daddy died and all of my decorations are still in deep storage from the move. Just never had time to get them out and then it was too late, you know?"

She opened the door then crossed back past him quickly as he stared on in confusion.

She threw her designer bag in the diaper bag and slung that over her shoulder, grabbed the tray of cookies, stuffed a small blanket under her arm then dangled the car seat in her three free fingers, as the other fingers balanced the house keys to lock the door. "Darius?" She hollered down the hallway. "It's time. Bring Andre."

"Hey." Marcus stepped toward her.

Alyson stopped and looked at him, then looked behind her. "What? Did I forget something?"

"Yeah. That I've got two hands here." He flashed jazz hands then took the car seat from her and walked toward the door shaking his head.

She was so used to doing it all she couldn't even see help when it was right in front of her.

❦

Alyson clicked her seatbelt, ignoring the fact she could feel Marcus's presence next to her. He radiated heat. And something made her heartbeat sound in her ears. "Okay. Now we have to go back to your place and pick up your bag, right?"

"Yeah, and some gifts."

She started backing out of the driveway before he even had his seatbelt on. Her skin tingled, and her breathing was shallow. Why did being close to him make her so nervous? It was getting worse with familiarity, not better. And he was just a guy. Just a friendly guy.

She needed to cool it, or their new friendship would signal the wrong type of relationship to her boys. She didn't need that awkwardness in her life, and she certainly didn't want them confused.

Even so, she couldn't wait to see where he lived.

He directed the way and not two minutes later they pulled into his driveway. "Oh my goodness! You're in the McGovern house. I used to play here as a kid. They—now you—have the biggest oak in the neighborhood. That's good luck!"

"Is it? I mean, it's lucky I have no grass so I don't have to mow."

"I wonder whatever happened to Jessie. We lost touch when we went to public school."

"You should look her up." He undid his seat belt and opened his door. "You want to come in?"

"Oh, I don't know." She faked. "We're already behind schedule."

Darius threw off his seatbelt and scrambled out of the backseat, leaving the door open in his haste to get to the front door.

"Well, that answers that." Marcus chuckled and got out of the car. Instead of heading straight for the door, though, he stopped to unbuckle a complainy, squirmy Andre behind him and help him out of the car seat.

The simple act tore at her heart. A complete stranger was a better daddy than their father. Will had always left their care to her no matter what else she had to do.

She reined in her angst and followed them to the door, intent on keeping neutral, calm, lest her boys think something was wrong. It always got her like this—one moment she was fine, the next she was in the depths of self-pity. She pushed it down.

Entering the house, it amazed her how different it was now. The old all-white living room Mrs. McGovern would never let them play in was now a deep red with a huge flat screen and multiple gaming consoles taking up most of one wall.

The other walls gleamed with instruments on hooks and shelves and in shadow boxes. Old brass horns, ancient dusty accordions, and others she couldn't name. More instruments in stands filled the corners. She recognized an old lyre in an elegantly carved shadow box.

"Wow!"

Darius expressed exactly what she'd been thinking. "Wow is right! What a cool collection."

Marcus flipped the light switch, and the room lit up with multi-colored Christmas lights in addition to a 1970s-style swooping silver floor lamp that hung right above the large leather couch.

"You get cool points for that retro lamp too. Seriously."

"Awesome. Didn't know I was being scored."

"Have you *met* me?"

He laughed and walked further into the house.

She followed. Their houses had a similar layout even though they looked totally different on the outside. His dining room and kitchen were about what she would expect from a bachelor. The countertop acted as a pantry, and gifts, wrapping paper tubes, tape and scissors covered the table. And that was just the layer of stuff she could see.

"I'm a bit of a slob. Do I lose points for that?"

"No. You're a creative type. It's just part of your whole mystique."

"I have mystique? No kidding."

His beaming smile was infectious, and she stood there smiling back, unable to look away. He broke their shared gaze and started piling up the presents to carry out.

Plink-plink-bong. A piano sounded from the family room farther in the house.

"Darius! Ask permission before you touch Mr. Powell's piano."

"It's all right. He can't hurt it." He put the gifts down and led her toward Darius. "Hey, show your mom what you've learned." Then to her he said, "We did some keyboard work after school. He knows his notes and scales, even a few songs."

Darius stood in front of a baby grand piano, with the bench pushed out of his way. Andre crawled under the bench.

"This is the biggest keyboard I've ever seen, Mr. Powell! Can we get one like this for school?"

"Sorry, buddy. Not in the budget." He stood on the other side of Darius and crossed his arms, leaning back like a coach. "Teach your mom something you've learned. Anything." He leaned forward and poked a key. "That's C."

"Oh yeah. I knew that." Darius started playing a robust version of "Hot Cross Buns," hitting the keys hard.

When he finished, she clapped and hugged him. "That's great, honey! I had no idea you could play piano!"

"I'm not done yet, Mom. That was the happy one. Now this one." He played a halting, almost eerie version of the same song. "See, Mom. You can change how a song *feels* if you change the key. *The key is the key*. Right, Mr. Powell?" Her son's pride and confidence shone like sunshine.

His teacher radiated pride as well and offered a fist bump. "There it is, my little man."

"Wow." She looked back at her son's smile. Then a realization hit her. He'd had four months of free music lessons. Free music therapy. She owed Marcus so much. "That's pretty advanced, isn't it?"

"He's a natural."

"Yeah, it's called major and minor. The major keys sound like fun and courage and the minor keys sound lonely."

"I'm . . . I'm amazed." She ran her hand over her son's short hair. He smiled smugly up at her. "Who is this maestro? I don't know where he gets it. I don't have a musical bone in my body."

"You have ear drums." Darius snickered.

"Well, yes, Mr. Smarty Pants, I do have ear drums."

Darius laughed and rolled his eyes. "Oh, Mom." Then he rousted his brother from under the bench by slithering toward him on the floor. Andre said "No!" and came to her to be held. She grunted as she picked him up—he was getting so big already.

Her gaze fell on Marcus who watched her. She didn't know how to thank him for all he'd done for Darius, for her family. She looked down at the keys, suddenly shy, and pressed two high ones—lonely, indeed. The hollow reverberation echoed in her heart.

Marcus came around her, bending toward her slightly as he reached to the keys, playing two strong notes. Those she felt vibrate low through her middle. *There must be something wrong with me if I'm so easily affected by him.* She forced herself to keep breathing steadily. But she shifted Andre from her hip to holding him in front of her, like an amulet to ward off attraction.

"How do you like my man cave?"

Her breath came out all at once in a nervous laugh. "Very un-cavelike. Most caves don't include a baby grand, you know." She took a few steps away, farther into the room. "I'm glad you kept it as it was. I always loved the real wood paneling and beams, and the stone fireplace."

"Are you kidding? This room is the whole reason I chose this house. It's the *ultimate* man cave." He grunted like an animal, which set off Darius to grunting and giggling. Andre bounced in her arms and she set him down.

"When I was a kid we'd pretend it was a great medieval hall. Amy was always the princess and Jessie and I would rock-paper-scissors to see who got to be the knight and who the evil sorcerer. Jessie's wolfhound was the dragon we chased. Sweetest dragon ever. And this room always smelled of her father's cherry pipe tobacco." She could almost see her young self, wearing an old curtain as a cape, running after the dog.

"Mo-o-om, when are we goooiiinnng? I want to be there already."

"Sorry. Mommy's being boring again. Come help." She motioned for Darius to grab some presents to carry to the car.

"Never boring." Marcus picked up several gifts again.

She glanced his way wondering if she'd heard him right.

"Working with you the past few weeks . . . never boring." Marcus's voice trailed off as he walked through the house toward the front door. "The more I know about you, the more I *want* to know."

Alyson stood blinking for a moment. That tone of voice—that was flirting, right? Or was it? Was he just being nice again, not letting her talk bad about herself? She sighed. No. It was flirting. She hoped she had the courage to end this before it began, for his sake if not for hers.

She followed the boys out of the house, her arms full of gifts for strangers. Her heart full of resolve to avoid what could only end badly.

Chapter Six

Marcus leaned toward her in the cramped confines of the Mercedes. Not that the space was small, but she hadn't been able to get used to being so close to him. Especially when he turned to look at the kids in the backseat and she caught a faint hint of a deep spicy musk. And another familiar scent she wanted more of. She wanted to bury her nose in his neck.

"They're asleep." He settled back in his seat.

"Long car ride. Works every time."

"You okay driving at night? We can switch."

She glanced at him with a knowing look. "You just want to drive."

"True."

"When we get to Katy, let's switch. It'll be easier if you drive us through Houston."

"Deal."

After a moment of silence, she said, "May I ask you a personal question?"

He chuckled. "You don't have to ask if you can ask. Just ask."

"How long have you been collecting instruments? Your collection is phenomenal. And what was that tall, stringed thing in the corner?"

"Sitar. My gramps traveled the world as a jazz and blues man. It's more popular overseas. Taken for granted here where commercial pop is king. It's his collection. Began it in his twenties and collected for a lifetime." He turned to her, and she glanced at him as much as she could while driving.

"Three-quarters of it went to museums in N'awlins and St. Lou. I inherited the ones too personal to sit in a warehouse. Each one has a story."

He shifted in his seat and stared straight ahead.

"Well?" She glanced at him a few times. "You can't just announce there's a story and not tell it."

His half-lidded eyes and cheeky grin told her he was teasing.

"Just gauging your interest. Which one you want to know about? The sitar?"

"The lyre. It looked pretty old. It was extra special to your grandfather, wasn't it?"

"Very." He shifted in his seat again.

She glanced and saw he was studying her openly. "Gramps won that lyre in a poker game in Dublin on his honeymoon. It was his prized possession because it marked a momentous occasion. The Irishman gave it to him with a blessing: 'May you always have music in your heart.' And he always did. Until the end."

He stared out the window.

She let silence rule the cab. The dark exterior and far-off taillights made it feel like they were alone out here. Like no one existed but them.

Marcus leaned over once again to peek in the back, and she gasped. He looked right at her, too close, and she glanced into his amber eyes but quickly returned her gaze to the road, where it was safe. This was going to be a rough holiday if her heart beat like this every time he came near.

"Didn't mean to scare you." He looked away again. "Since the boys are asleep, you want to keep listening to whispers of fish searching for Dory or would you like some tunes?"

She was so used to that background noise it hadn't even registered. "Yes, please. There are CDs in the glove box. Something relaxing, so it doesn't wake them."

"Madame Captain." He affected a stiff accent, not quite British. "I am your Navigator and Communications Officer. Allow me."

He plugged a flash drive into a USB port in the dash, then fiddled with buttons, skipping selections until relaxing piano, that reminded her of a babbling brook or falling leaves, filled the car.

"That's beautiful."

He said nothing but smiled.

They listened quietly through several short pieces—all solos—guitar, violin, saxophone, standing bass, drums, each playing the same melody as the first. "This is a demo, isn't it?"

"Yep."

"For your band?" She had thought he was in a rock band, not jazz.

"No, this is solo work. Just me. Just to show my instrumental range. I have another set to show the range of musicality for each instrument but that gets too swinging to play right now." He thumbed to the back, indicating the kids.

"Marcus, if I didn't know you better, I'd think you were showing off."

He bowed his head but continued to grin. "Guilty as charged."

"What are you doing here? Why aren't you in New York or L.A. or even Nashville?"

"All in good time. I'll make it to Hollywood someday. I want to write movie scores."

"Movie scores?"

"Yeah. I've arranged music for local theater and a video game company, but Hollywood is where it's at. That's where I want to be. I mean, I'm sure I'll have to put in my time there as a session man before anyone will let me write and produce. But I'm building for the long game, so I'm ready for that." Even though his words sounded cautious, he burned with enthusiasm.

"How does a normal person even break into that business? Don't you need contacts?"

"Well, yeah. I'm trying to get enough work under my belt, create an awesome video profile. At some point I'll have to do the footwork in person, you know? Get a foot in the door. Literally."

She knew about the videos. She'd gone searching after overhearing him tell Bertie that the Singing Elf videos had gotten cross-linked to his band's videos. Instead of his band, she'd found more solo work. And she'd binge-watched them all.

But she'd never tell *him* that. He'd think she was a stalker. She didn't *want* to be interested, it could only complicate life, force a mirror onto how lonely she was, but she couldn't help herself.

"Wow, I'm impressed. With your planning as much as your skill." She glanced his way, smiling casually, but her breath caught in her throat when his amber eyes met hers.

She stared at the dark road ahead and cleared her throat. "You're set on Hollywood? I have a few friends, well, I'm not sure if they're still my friends after the divorce, but I might have some contacts for the New York scene. A few agents. Maybe they could talk to you and give you some ideas on how to break in."

He crossed his arms and stared out the window again.

"You should have an agent—or are they called managers in the music biz? Whatever they're called, you need representation. You're that good."

"How would *you* know?"

"Well, that was rude." She tried to glare at him and failed since he didn't bother looking her way.

"For your information, Mr. Poopypants, I may have been a housewife when I lived in New York, but I took lessons at one of the premiere dance studios, even taught there, and I heard a lot about what went on with stage actors and pit musicians trying to make it on Broadway.

"I mean, my *best friend* was an agent exclusively for actors wanting chorus positions. She was always at the studio trying to get new accounts. You have to play the game. It may be creative, but it's still a business.

"Undiscovered talent stays undiscovered. That's what reps are for. You're the talent. It's too hard to be both. Get a rep." She hadn't meant to speak so vehemently, but she meant every word.

There was a moment of silence before he said, "Sorry, I asked."

"I'm not." She glanced at him and met his gaze a moment. Tortured artist type, moody, broody eyes. She had to force her gaze back to the road. "Friendship is telling each other when you're out of bounds. You told me I needed to accept help. Well, you need to stop second-guessing your talent."

Her words hovered in the air. Her next breath held fast in her chest, anticipating his angry reaction. Anger that never came. She could kick herself for expecting him to react like her ex-husband. They were opposites in every way but physique. No, even that was different. Will was leaner overall, even a couple inches shorter. Marcus was a gentle giant.

The *Star Wars* theme song rang loudly in the car. He shifted his large frame to get to his phone from his belt, the confines unforgiving to his elbows.

She shook her head at how much of a nerd this ultra-talented man was, but the movie theme song—score—made perfect sense knowing what she now knew about his dreams.

He glanced at the phone before answering. "Hey, Mama."

"Where're you at? Supper's almost over."

Alyson could hear the woman's strong Southern accent clearly. It sounded like she was yelling into her phone.

"We're going to be late getting in. Don't worry about us for dinner." Silence on the other end. "Mama? You still there?"

"How many is this *we*?"

"Uncle Mason didn't tell you? I talked to him just this morning. He said he'd pass it along."

"He told me your *girlfriend* is selling him her car, but honey, I didn't know you were bringing her for the week."

Alyson smacked his arm.

"Ow!"

"You didn't tell her?" She mouthed the words putting as much anger into the mime as possible. "I'm going to kill you!" She choked the air with her right hand.

Marcus laughed.

"Who're you talking to, Marcus?" Darius's sleepy voice mumbled from the back. Probably awakened by the slap and the '*ow*,' so it was her own doing.

"I'm talking to my mama. You want to say hi? Tell her your name and age. Wait a second." He switched it to speaker-phone. "Okay, now."

"Hellooo, Mrs. Powell," Darius sang like he was greeting a teacher in the morning. "My name is Darius, and I turned eight last week."

"Last month, baby," Alyson corrected.

"I'm not a baby, Mom. I'm eight now. Andre's the baby."

"Not a baby!" Andre yelled.

"Andre. Andre. Tell my mama how old you are."

"No!"

Marcus's mom laughed. "Well, he must be two."

"Yes, ma'am. And I'm Alyson Stefanelli Daniels. Thank you for allowing us to visit, and I'm so sorry for the short notice. I promise we won't be any trouble." She hit Marcus again, striking his ribs, and this time he laughed and jerked away as if she'd tickled him. It jostled the whole car, and she tightened her grip on the steering wheel.

He took the phone off speaker and put it back to his ear, still chuckling.

"So that's who's who."

"Baby, she sounds flat. Like a news anchor or weather girl or something. Where's she from?"

Alyson heard every word. She wished she hadn't. To be disliked before you even meet . . .

"There will be plenty of time for questions later, Mama. We'll see you around 9-ish. Love you." He hung up.

"I can't believe you." Alyson seethed.

"What?"

"You didn't even tell her we were coming."

"It's no big deal."

"It is to me." She poked the power button on the stereo system, replacing his music with tense silence. "You better be glad I'm driving and have to pay attention to the road, Marcus."

"Got a temper, do you?"

"I'm Irish-Italian. Of course I have a temper! Why are you even doing this? What do you get out of it? And don't say a ride. It's got to be more than that."

"I see 500 kids ages five to twelve every week," he said casually. "Temper tantrums don't work with me."

Her boiling blood cooled immediately, surprised by his calm response. Her ex would have yelled back, and they would have fought over every little nothing the rest of the night.

Quick as a snap, she saw her part in the demise of their marriage. Will had begun ignoring them, working all the time. The only way she could get him to engage with her was to pick fights. Nothing else got his attention. And it had only hastened the fall. Her stomach flopped, and acid churned.

"Besides, I don't need a reason to help a friend. God commands we help where we can."

Oh great, and now he's playing the God card. What little anger was left in her fizzled out. There was nothing to argue. She felt like a fool.

She thought of all the presents he'd bought on his last day of work, a day he hadn't even been scheduled for—surely he hadn't planned on taking those gifts on the Greyhound bus with him. Yes, what he got out of this was a ride—so he could deliver presents just like a real-life St. Nick. She could kick herself. "I'm sorry, Marcus."

"Don't worry about it."

"Well, there is one thing still to worry about."

"What's that?"

"Your mom thinks I'm your girlfriend."

His phone went off again, this time with the *Star Wars* cantina band song. He held up a finger and muttered an apology as he answered.

"Hey, Gordie! . . . No, headed out of town. Let me get you Joaquin's number. Hang on." While Marcus scrolled through his contacts, the man on the other end kept talking. "Joaquin's no good as a session man! I need guitar *and* trumpet on this. When are you coming back? Maybe I can wait. You're the best session man in the city, bro."

"Not till January. It's on the calendar." He poked the screen. "Okay, you have Joaquin's digits in a text."

"You're not cheating on me are you, man? You're not cutting a Christmas album in Houston, are you?"

"What are you talking about?"

"I saw you on YouTube, man. We should do the Christmas album *together*. Those things fly off the shelves."

"It's family time, Gordie. Merry Christmas."

Alyson could hear the irritation in Marcus's voice and realized how rarely he sounded that way. What had set him off?

"It'll be merry if I can find a trumpet player. See you in January, my friend." The call ended.

"Mr. Powell? What's a session man?"

It didn't surprise Alyson that Darius was listening in rather than turning the DVD player back on. He was always trying to listen in on adult conversations. Just like she had when she was his age.

Marcus turned in the seat to look at Darius, once again getting close enough to lay his head on her shoulder if he'd wanted to.

"I work in a studio when I'm not teaching. A recording studio. Every time you record music it's called a recording session, that's where it gets the funny name. Session musician. Session man."

Whatever that manly scent was that drove her crazy—she could only smell it when he was close like this. Dare she take a big whiff now?

"Can I go there? I want to see it."

"Huh. That'd be a fun field trip, wouldn't it? I'll ask when we get back to school."

She leaned slightly toward him and breathed in as he sat back.

"Did you just sniff me?" Marcus's normally deep voice climbed higher with every word.

"Don't be absurd. That's just silliness."

"You did. I heard it."

Darius giggled in the back seat.

She glanced at Marcus guiltily. "I was trying to figure out what scent is in your cologne, is all."

"You like it?"

She shrugged her shoulders. "It's nice. It suits you. It's really familiar too." She surely wasn't going to admit that it had been driving her nuts with desire for the last hour and a half.

She wished she had worn her hair down so it could hide her face. Or at least it could disrupt her peripheral vision so she couldn't see when Marcus watched her. Maddening. *A change in topic—need a change in topic!*

"That Christmas album isn't a bad idea."

Marcus relaxed into his seat and stared out the window, replacing the intensity in the car with a feeling of irritation again. Why did that bother him so much?

She poked at it, as the distance was good for them. "An agent or manager would tell you it's a smart idea to do that album. Any way to get your name out there. Royalties on holiday music last a lifetime—a few months of the year anyway. And movies and TV shows are always looking for holiday songs they can get on the cheap because they produce holiday shows every year. And then you'd have a national market. Something you should think about."

"Christmas album doesn't fit the image I'm going for."

"What image is that?"

"Serious musician. I don't want to forever be seen in a Santa suit. Or an elf costume for that matter. Thanks a lot, YouTubers."

"And serious musician has to be ... what? Undiscovered? Poor?"

"I don't have the right schools or classes on my degree to impress anybody. I can't have my first real success be Christmas rock for the mall crowd. That's all anybody will see me as. I would have thought a woman like you, wearing brand-name everything, would understand a little more about image and branding. You've got to look the part or people pass on by."

"*A woman like me*?" Her ire was up instantly. She toned it down for Darius's sake, talking low. "A woman like me? Look the part? I have all this stuff because my ex bought it for me—and I bought into it, too, for a while. He was the one who cared about his *image* more than he cared about—" *his family*. She glanced at Darius in the rear-view but couldn't tell what he was thinking. She tried not to bad-mouth their father in front of them. After everything they'd been through, she didn't want to traumatize them any further. So she swallowed her anger. "Image isn't nearly as important as dignity."

Silence.

Was Marcus more like her ex than she thought? Caring elementary school teacher today, but at the first sign of success he'd run away and perfect his musician's public image, wouldn't he? Fast living and late hours. She could never be with a musician.

Come on, Alyson, he's just a guy, and this is just a transaction. You're buying a car, not looking for a man. Just a transaction. A temporary thing. She'd never have to see him again after this weekend except maybe at a parent-teacher conference.

"Can you do me a favor?" His voice was low, calm. "Don't tell my family I worked at the mall. If they knew about it, they'd never let me live it down."

"Yeah, sure. I get it." Yep, he was just like her ex. Image was everything. God forbid if he tried to be honest. Why was she always attracted to jerks?

৵৹৻

Marcus tried to think of something to say to lessen the distance between them. A wall that wasn't there before was now built high and wide. He didn't know what he'd said, but when she brought her ex into it, he knew to back off and shut up.

His sister, divorced for two years now, was still rage-filled at the mention of her ex or any memory of him that surfaced. A closed-in car and a three-hour drive wasn't the place to bring out that kind of divorcée rage.

He asked to turn on the radio and found an oldies station. He sang along, pretending everything was all right, and eventually she relaxed and sang along too. Four Seasons, Elvis, Gladys Knight, even Willie Nelson—there wasn't a song she didn't know the words to.

She had a strong mid-toned voice, not as high as he expected. He wanted to test her against his music collection, see how much they had in common.

Even though she sang along, he got the feeling she was still somehow reserved—like she was pretending she was alone in the car. She kept her eyes focused on the road though he knew she could probably see him watching in her peripheral vision. She avoided him on purpose.

Image is not as important as dignity. There was so much hurt behind that simple statement, but nothing he could touch or undo.

Chapter Seven

Alyson was glad she'd given Marcus the reins at their last stop. There were so many twists and turns in his parents' neighborhood. It was dark, already past nine. The streets were so wide she couldn't see street names until they were passing them.

But even better than the super-wide streets were all the amazing Christmas lights! The kind of lights people paid a service to install. 'Best Lighting Display' boasted a small sign in the yard they'd just passed—sheets of string lights hanging from tall trees, like sparkling waterfalls.

Wide streets and large lawns, huge homes, but not the McMansion style—each one was unique, the architecture highlighted by the Christmas lights or dramatic uplighting. There was wealth here for sure. Homes this size, with this much yard, would go for a mighty high price in Houston.

She wished it didn't make her feel inferior, but it did. She'd had a beautiful home in New York. Now, she couldn't even afford a low income apartment on her own.

"We're late, but just in time. The candlelight service is my favorite."

"Marcus, are you sure it's okay for us to stay with your family? Should we go to a hotel for the night?"

"No room at the inn on Christmas Eve, you know that." He pulled up to the curb and turned off the car. "Besides, we're here, and all the lights are on to welcome us."

She studied his house, taking a deep breath. It was so covered in religious and Santa decorations she couldn't see much else. Lights, lights everywhere, the entire lawn was a maze of lights and decorations—lollipops, candy canes, even a mini choo-choo. The children were exclaiming each as she was seeing them. Darius kept saying, "Look, Mom!" and announcing a new thing. "How many Santas are there? I can't keep track!"

"Well, what do you think?" Marcus asked.

Alyson giggled at how over-the-top it all was. "I think their electricity bill must be astounding. I bet you can see this from space."

"I know it's a little much, but since they started the competition, Mom's gone for 'Most Outrageous' every year. Looks like someone beat her this time, though."

She pointed to the award sign stuck next to a sign that said, 'North Pole.' "Nope. Looks like she got it."

"Yes! Reigning champ!" He pumped his fist. "That's my mama! Come on, let's get inside."

Darius was out first and trying out the maze. Andre screamed to be let out of his car seat and kicked at her once he was free, turning to jelly and sliding to the pavement. He ran after his brother.

"Darius! Andre! Get back here, don't you dare damage those decorations!"

"It's okay. The judging is done, they can't do any harm."

"Marcus, I'm surprised the whole shebang isn't falling over or exploding at this very moment. Seconds, it takes mere seconds, for them to destroy stuff."

Marcus laughed and lifted their bags out of the hatchback. Looking at the front door he said, "I'm surprised no one's come out to greet us yet."

She tried to grab the bags, but Marcus ignored her attempt and started rolling them up the walk to the warmly lit front door.

"I'll get the presents on a second trip," he said over his shoulder.

She grabbed the cookies she'd made and followed him up the walkway. "Come on, boys." Nothing. Like they didn't even hear her. "Darius, Andre, come here, please."

"Darius, come meet my mom."

Darius flew to them, Andre following in his wobbly way.

"Nicely done."

"A new stimulus is always better than a command. Try keeping the attention of a whole classroom at a time." He grinned and opened the door.

Somewhere in the house, out of sight, a child screeched the cry of mild pain but abject terror. A variety of adults swooped into action, some soothing, some scolding another child.

She stepped into a large foyer. The scents of cookies and a wood fire reached her almost simultaneously. No one noticed them come in, still concerned over the owie of one child and punishment of another.

Andre joined in the crying of the other young children, and Alyson had to pick him up with one arm, while holding the tray of cookies with the other. Darius marched forward, probably hoping to join the melee.

An older, pear-shaped woman with close-cropped salt and pepper hair, ambled toward them. She seemed tired, moving as though she ached, but with a great big smile for her boy. "Marcus, my baby! You made it."

A host of others came to the door then too. Their smiles not hiding the fact that when they first saw her, each and every one of them hesitated, their faces going stiff for a second, probably shocked Marcus had brought home a white girl.

The crowd surrounded them, hugs for Marcus, and light teasing about how he was always late. The family was huge. Not only were there more people than she could count, but most of them were several inches taller and wider than she was, even the women. She felt like a child.

Andre had stopped crying long enough to take a look around at all the people but began again, grabbing her neck with a death grip as soon as someone tried to lift him from her.

Instead, a woman with blonde, copper, and black braids took the tray of cookies from her. The relief to her wrist was immediate. "Thank you." She shifted Andre to her left hip, freeing her right hand for introductions.

The woman took her hand and gave it a short, vigorous shake. "I'm Gail."

"How do you do? I'm Alyson Stefanelli Daniels."

Gail's grin stretched wider still. "'*How do you do?*' Aren't you cute? So you're my brother's main squeeze."

"Gail, don't antagonize the poor girl." Marcus's mom took Alyson's hand in her left one, using her right to rub Andre's back while he scowled at everyone tearfully, burrowing into Alyson's neck.

"Welcome, Alyson, dear."

Darius appeared between them, pulling on Marcus's mom's arm.

"And who are you?" She bent down to Darius's level.

"I'm Darius, of course."

She laughed and cupped his cheek. "Of *course* you are!"

Alyson loved the woman's ever-ready smile and good cheer.

"This is the boy I told you about, Mom."

Alyson watched Marcus and his mom share a look. She couldn't tell what passed between them, but in a flash, she understood that this invitation really had nothing to do with her and everything to do with Darius being Marcus's pet project.

He'd obviously told his mom about working with Darius in the after-school program, had told her about his turn around. The look they shared was a serious one.

Marcus's mom touched her son's cheek as if he were fragile. "So glad you're home, baby." She did the same to Darius. "Dear boy, you can call me Mama Dottie. Why don't you run and play with the others?"

Darius didn't need any more of an invitation. There was a group of boys his age waiting outside the circle of adults, and Darius ran off with them as

Marcus and Alyson were ushered to the kitchen, a small crowd following, others staying in the foyer talking.

The kitchen was brightly lit and shades of yellow, orange and brown, the colors of perpetual harvest. Many trays of cookies, bars, cakes, and quick breads lined the long counter. The trays and stands were gay reds and greens, blues and silver. The clash was glorious and homey.

But just as Alyson was about to compliment the beauty of the large and well-appointed kitchen and all the rich-looking desserts, an angry old woman hollered. "Milton! Who is that? Why's a stranger in my house? What does she want?"

"Hey, *Grandmere*, it's me, Marcus." He bent close to her at the kitchen table, just inches from her face, and smiled gently.

The use of French surprised Alyson.

"Milton?" The old woman's fear switched to a resigned sadness. "Marcus. Where have you been? Are you getting good grades?"

"*Grandmere*, this is my friend Alyson, she's from San Antonio."

"Oooh! I like San Antonio." She sounded like a child now. "Milty loved playing there at the Menger."

"Yeah, *Grandmere*, this is Alyson." He motioned for Alyson to come closer.

The woman finally took notice of her again. And didn't look pleased. She squinted her baggy-lidded eyes almost closed.

"Why, she's white as white can be. White as my hair." That tickled her, and she laughed until she wheezed. Others in the room chuckled.

"*Maman*," Dorothy scolded. "That's not her fault now, is it?"

Marcus snorted laughter.

Andre fussed again and squirmed toward the cookies, his hands outstretched. "Down! Want down! Want cookie!"

"Alyson, honey,"—Mama Dottie took Andre out of her arms—"this boy's almost as big as you are."

Andre seemed shocked at first but melted against the large, soft woman, cookies forgotten.

Alyson wiped a thin layer of sweat from her neck where her son had laid his hot little head. "Almost as heavy too. Big for his age, but still clingy for two."

"Milty, is that little Marcus?"

Alyson glanced at Marcus in time to see his face fall. "*Grandmere*. I'm Marcus." Then to his mom, "She's gotten worse."

"Much. It's been real hard here lately."

"Yeah, Marcus," Gail nibbled on one of Alyson's cherry almond cookies. "It would've been nice to have your help. You know I hate setting up decorations."

Andre saw Gail's cookie and lunged for it. Dottie put him down, and he came back to stand behind Alyson's leg.

"Who is this?" The grandmother's fearful tone was back.

"*Grandmere*, this is my friend, Alyson."

"What does she *want*?"

"What all of us want, *Grandmere*. To be loved and welcome." He kissed the top of his grandmother's head. Then he crossed to his mom and did the same. "I'm so sorry, Mama."

"It's nothing." But her voice and her eyes were teary.

Alyson bowed her head, wishing she wasn't the cause of the old woman's alarm. They shouldn't have come here.

Gail turned to her, blocking the grandmother's suspicious glare. "What kind of cookies are these?"

"Shortbread, cherry almond, and pignolis— Italian pine nut cookies."

"They're not very sweet. Are they diet cookies?" Her wrinkled nose said she didn't think much of them.

"No. Made with real butter and sugar." She tried not to sound disappointed that they hated her cookies. Bland like her. "We have them with tea Christmas morning in my family."

"We'll put them out tomorrow with the others," Gail said, taking another pignoli from the tray. "I'll have to make room."

Alyson followed Gail's gaze to the myriad cookies on the long countertop bar, all rich and caramel and chocolate and toasted coconut. Her own cookies could not compare to these rich flavors. She sighed. At least she hadn't come empty-handed.

The grandmother sighed loudly. "I'm tired, Dorothy."

"Yes, *Maman*, we'll get you to bed." Dottie signaled to a middle-aged woman who went to the grandmother.

"Where are you all sleeping?" Gail asked Marcus point-blank. She took a bite of the cookie. "Need an air mattress in your old room for the boys?" Her eyebrow could not get any higher, her implication clear.

"Smooth, Gail. Smooth. I'll sleep in the den. They can have my room."

"We're just friends." No one heard her correction because everyone started talking at once. Dottie admonished her daughter Gail for being tactless, and Marcus's other sister, Justine, introduced herself and listed off the names of her children. Gail hated on her cookies.

"This is a different taste." Gail gave the other half of the pignoli to her sister who ate it and gave a thoughtful "hhm."

She met uncles and cousins and more cousins, some referring to their spouses or children who weren't even in the room. There were so many names thrown at her she wasn't even sure of her own anymore, and a dull headache landed right on top of her head.

Dottie patted her shoulder. "Y'all leave her alone, now. Give 'em time to get settled." The small crowd dispersed, chatting and laughing. "Alyson, dear, you look a little peaked. Have you eaten? I can warm up a plate for you."

"I'm fine, thank you." She lied. She was starving.

Marcus led them to his old room and wasn't surprised to see his mom hadn't changed a thing. Nothing ever changed in this house. Everyone just aged in place—same old, same old.

"You have a Jack-and-Jill bathroom right through there"—he pointed to the far door—"and there are extra blankets and pillows in the closet. Is the queen bed going to be enough for the three of you or should I get a cot or sleeping bag for Darius?"

"It's fine. Thank you." But the venom dripping from her voice told him nothing was fine.

"What's wrong?"

"We're not guests, Marcus, we're party crashers. Your family resents having us here. We're an imposition. Why would you do that?" She was near tears.

"Whoa. Whoa, now. No tears." He held her shoulders gently and bent back and down, trying to see her face, to meet her downcast gaze. "It's no big deal. Really. It's okay."

"Don't you try to comfort me!" She backed out of his grasp. "I'm mad at you. I'm frustrated. We should have just stayed home and been miserable on our own. Now I'm going to make everyone else miserable." She sat on the bed with a huff. "Your poor sweet mom has enough to deal with already without adding a bunch of strangers. We should've stayed home."

Darius breezed into the room but whatever exciting thing he was about to exclaim died as he saw his mom's frown. His immediate concern was touching—no doubt he'd seen her in all kinds of emotional states over the past year. *No one's happy if Mama ain't happy.*

"Hey." Marcus sat next to her on the bed and gave her a friendly sideways hug. "I don't know where this is coming from, but I do know you've been burning the candle at both ends for as long as I've known you. This is your vacation. Relax. There're no schedules to work out or registers to balance, no customers to help. Just relax. Okay?"

He gave her another quick squeeze, then stood. "I'll be back in a minute. Darius, come give me a hand?"

The boy perked up immediately, happy for something to do. Andre patted his mom's knees and climbed up. She held him.

"Darius, sweetie. Remember your manners, please."

"Yes, ma'am."

Marcus looked back at her, about to say Darius could relax his manners in this rambunctious house, but caught her rocking Andre, her eyes closed, her features soft and completely in the moment. Only love for her son shone, and she was radiant.

It was a moment before he could tear his eyes away from her and close the door. When he did, he caught the huge, sparkly-eyed smile of Darius. He knew what that smile was saying.

"You like my mom. Like, *like-like*."

"Keep it quiet, kid." He rubbed Darius's head. "Let's go to the kitchen. I know exactly what your mom needs."

೪~೪

Alyson lay her sleeping toddler down on his side and placed the pillow next to him on the bed so he couldn't roll off. She had calmed herself by calming her boy. It always worked that way. When she focused on her sons and on providing loving care and guidance, she was at her best. She was at her worst when she thought about money and felt abandoned, trapped, and stupid.

Alyson took a deep breath and willed herself back to calmness. This may be a bad Christmas for her, but it could still be a good one for her boys if she allowed it to be and stopped getting upset at little things that didn't matter. So what if they didn't like her cookies. The important thing was that she hadn't come empty-handed. She had done the right thing even if the result was less than spectacular.

And Marcus was right. Now that she was away from work where she had to keep it together and wear a smile all the time, she was losing it, on edge. She needed this break more than she cared to admit.

A soft knock. A giggle—Darius. She went to open the door, and Marcus walked in with a glass of milk, hunched over, trying to make himself small.

Darius stood behind him covering his mouth with both hands to keep from laughing.

Marcus said in a high-pitched voice, "*Mija*, warm milk for you, *mija*, so you can sleep tonight." He meant it to be funny, but she was amazed by how well he imitated Luisa's speech. Darius cracked up behind his hands, laughing at his teacher's antics.

Marcus chuckled, too, a big kid himself. Watching Darius made him laugh even harder. He stood upright and handed her the glass.

"Oh! You did warm it! This is perfect."

He and Darius shared a fist bump.

"Thank you." She took a big sip, making sure to get plenty of milk on her lip because that always made Darius laugh too. She looked right at him, and he began a new round of chuckles, shaking his head at his silly mom. "What?"

"Uh, you have a little, uh . . ." Marcus didn't miss a beat, but played right along, one hand on his hip, the other pointing anxiously at her milk mustache.

"What? Oh, here?" She barely touched the corner of her lip. "Thanks."

"Oh, nooooo, Mooooom!" Darius fell on the floor in a heap of giggles.

Marcus pointed at her 'stache again, looking at her like a painter looks at a painting, stroking his chin in deep thought. She cleared another small spot. More giggles from the floor.

Marcus pointed a third time, and she chomped at his finger with a snort.

Marcus jumped back, eyes wide, cradling his hand close to his chest.

Darius laughed big belly laughs pointing at Marcus. "You fell for it!"

"I almost lost a finger! And you knew that was coming?"

Darius laughed and nodded.

"You couldn't warn a brother?"

More giggles.

But she heard a fretful cry from Andre, who'd been awakened by all the laughter. She wiped the milk from her lip and set the glass down. She sat on the bed and stroked his back until he settled into sleep again.

"Sorry," Marcus whispered.

Darius stood by his new partner in crime. "Yeah, sorry, Mom." He tried to whisper but hadn't mastered the art yet and just sounded loud and breathy.

"Are you boys coming?" She heard a female voice from the hallway and keys jangling.

"Are you asking or am I?" Darius looked up at Marcus with big puppy-dog eyes.

"Can Darius come to the candlelight service with us? All the little ones are asleep, but his age and older are going. Lots of music and singing. Prayer by candlelight. My sister Justine can watch over Andre if you want to come too."

"Are you sleepy, sweetheart?"

Darius opened his eyes as wide as he could—whites all around his big browns. "No, ma'am. Wide awake."

She put her hand out for him, and he came to her. She hugged him. "Go have fun. And obey Mr. Powell. No horseplay, understood?"

"Yes, ma'am. And ..." He slowly bowed his head.

"What is it?"

"The other boys are in bunk beds." His voice had taken on a petulant, almost sad quality, like he knew she was going to say no. "And they have a top bunk open."

"You want to be with them?"

"You won't have to wait up for him, then," Marcus offered. "You could get some rest."

"And if you ... *wake* in the night?"

Darius met her gaze. He'd been having night terrors ever since the divorce, but less and less. He'd been so clingy for so long . . .

"I'll be okay, Mom. I know where you are. I can find you."

It brought fresh tears to her eyes. "My brave boy." She kissed his forehead and hugged him again. "Go have fun. Tell me all about it tomorrow." She released him.

"Love you, Mom!" No sooner was he out of her arms than he was running past Marcus and into the hallway. "I'm coming!" Happy shouts rang back.

"He's already made friends?" She pressed her hands before her mouth like a prayer to cover her amazement. "This is wonderful. You don't understand . . ."

"I've watched him grow and change over the last four months."

"Yes, of course. And you've had so much to do with that. I . . . I can't thank you enough."

He bowed his head then looked in the direction Darius had run. He was such a handsome man, made even more so by his tender heart. The impact he'd had on Darius was a minor miracle.

Maybe that was the real reason he had invited them to Christmas with his family—because he knew Darius would have a good time with other kids his age instead of facing a whole vacation of boredom with Mom and baby brother.

By the sound of it, everyone was filing out the front door, kids laughing and talking, moms barking orders.

"Boys are pack animals at this age." Marcus watched the hubbub in the hall. "He's got a pack to run with now. They're good kids. He'll be fine."

"Thank you, Marcus. Thank you, thank you, thank you."

"It's nothing." He offered a closed-lip smile, seeming uncomfortable with the praise. He reached in for the door to close it.

"It's *everything* to me."

Their gaze met once again, and lingered. She tried to put all the gratitude she held in her heart into it—make him understand what he'd done for them. But something wasn't right. She couldn't read him. Her gratitude only seemed to embarrass him, cause him to turn away, to hide.

"Goodnight."

She was left staring at a shut door, more confused than ever about Marcus.

Chapter Eight

The smell of bacon and the sound of laughter from kids and adults awakened her from a dreamless sleep. Andre pulled her hair, and she took his little fist in hers. She couldn't believe she had slept so hard. Usually, the first night in a new place, every little sound woke her.

She removed the lock of hair from Andre's still-sleepy grasp and sat up. The shower turned on in the Jack-and-Jill bathroom.

She didn't know what to do. The voices outside her room all sounded joyful, greeting each other with "Merry Christmas." She wanted to hide in the room until it was all over. Crashing the family party had been a horrible idea. She wished she could fast-forward this part.

"Merry Christmas, Mrs. Powell." Darius's voice cut through the general chatter.

"You can call me Mama Dottie, sweet boy."

"Merry Christmas, Mama Dottie." She could hear the huge smile in her son's voice as he came closer to her door.

He didn't knock, but barged right in, leaving the door open. "Mom! Mom! Mom! Come on! We're going to miss it!"

"Okay. We'll be right there." Darius didn't bother waiting and zoomed back out as quickly as he'd come in. She looked longingly at the Jack-n-Jill bathroom, the shower still running, and decided to just get dressed. She couldn't shower now anyway.

Holding Andre's hand, Alyson walked softly into the great room at the back of the house, feeling like an interloper. She saw that everyone else was in their jammies and robes. Younger kids sat on the floor near the tree, tearing into their gifts, even as one of the tween girls continued to deliver gifts to the adults sitting on every available surface, including folding chairs.

She saw Darius up front with the other boys. She got his attention and tried to wave him back to stand with her—they should let the Powells have their family moment.

She felt someone come close.

Dottie stood just to the side. "Coffee 'n' biscuits on the counter, dear. Grab 'em while they hot."

"I'm sorry we were such a surprise last night."

"It's nothing. I'm glad you're here." She bent to greet Andre, and he turned to his mom's leg.

"Sorry. He takes a little while to warm up to people."

"He's shy like his mama?" Dottie smiled at her and rubbed Andre's head, patted his shoulder.

She wasn't shy but didn't think arguing the point was called for. She knew she wasn't acting normal—she just felt like such a loser for having to crash another family's party, for not bringing gifts, for being the odd man out. For accepting charity.

Maybe she could have sold the car another time, but she needed the money now. She could start the spring semester with just a late-registration fee and be that much closer to her goal. Or at least afford good daycare. She hated her future, whatever it was.

"Alyson shy? Impossible." Marcus came up behind them, then kissed and hugged his mom. "Merry Christmas, Mama."

Andre let go of Alyson and reached up to Marcus.

"Hey, little dude, want to open presents?" Marcus lifted Andre easily and carried him facing outward to the action, then sat on the floor with him on the outer ring of the kids. Andre livened up, laughing and clapping at the happy mayhem.

"He's so good with them. Andre doesn't trust just anybody." Maybe Andre loved Marcus so well because Darius loved him. He had really helped her son heal—Darius had been ready to self-destruct before he started coming home from school talking about Mr. Powell all the time.

If only she'd met his favorite teacher sooner. A different way. A different time. Not when she was at her most pathetic.

She felt a pat on her back and looked up to see Dottie smiling at her knowingly. *Uh-oh. What did that mean?*

"Why don't you go join them up close? You don't have to hang back."

"I don't want to intrude." What was the right thing to do as a Christmas guest?

Dottie pushed her forward, smiling warmly. "Go be part of the fun."

She sat with Marcus and Andre on the floor.

"Was hoping you'd join us." Marcus gave her a friendly hug on her shoulders.

She tucked her hair behind her ear to allow a better view of him. His soft smile made her feel pretty again, even with plain hair and no make-up.

"Hey, you eat yet?"

"No, we'll wait until everyone's had theirs."

"No, you've got to have the bacon and cheese biscuit while it's hot. Be right back." He got up gracefully for such a big guy and left.

Darius came out of the crowd of boys with a half-unwrapped xylophone for Andre, then popped back into the group.

Andre's pounding just added to the noisy joy surrounding them, so she allowed it.

Gail and the other sister she'd met last night—whose name she'd already forgotten—waved from their perch on the couch. A few people looked her way occasionally, not in a mean, gossipy way but in a 'who in the world is this white girl?' sort of way.

She was used to people—all people—being curious about her mixed family. The only time it bothered her was when people assumed her boys were adopted. Nothing charged her mama-bear defenses more.

Marcus came back and sat again, this time with a heaping Styrofoam plate of six biscuits in one hand and two coffees cradled against his chest. "Did I get it right? Two creams, one sugar?"

She nodded, a goofy grin on her face—she could feel it and closed her mouth. How did he know how she liked her coffee? She doubted her ex could have gotten it right, even after nine years of marriage. Taking the coffee he offered her, she reminded herself to breathe normally as he sat close enough for their knees to touch.

ﻬ

Marcus threw the football to his teenage nephew Jayden. He caught it and took not three steps before two younger nephews took Jayden out in a sandwich slam.

"We're not playing tackle!" Marcus hollered. The brothers laughed and helped their dazed cousin up from the ground. Marcus was about to go reprimand them when his dad called him over to the smoking grill.

As with any holiday, Dad, Uncle Mason, some of the older men of the family and a few widower neighbors sat with the grill and gossiped. They wouldn't call it gossip, but that didn't change what it was.

It was hard being the only man his age in the family—his brother was twelve years older, and the nearest male cousin ten years younger. He'd grown up surrounded by women, and his brother never let him forget it.

Marcus had lived years wondering when he would be able to join the men around the grill, but when that moment had finally come, he'd discovered it was dull and he'd wanted to be anywhere else. His older brother, Lawrence, used to get his goat by saying it was because Marcus was forever a child.

He'd rather be seen as a child than give up on living and having fun. 'Sitting with the grill' was for old men who barely moved. He never wanted to be like that.

"Hey, Mr. Clifford. Mr. Weiss. Good to see y'all again." He shook the neighbors' hands. "Yeah,

Dad?" He heard one of his cousins call his name, so he waved them on to play without him.

"I want to talk to you a minute."

"Sure thing." He had wondered when his dad would finally talk to him. They hadn't seen each other since July and not a word between them since. Marcus was waiting for an apology from that fight. Didn't expect one though.

"Dad, if this is about Sunday, I really don't want any part of it. I'm not preaching. Not even doing Children's Church. I mean it this time."

"Well, aren't you presumptuous? That's not what I want to talk to you about, son." His dad put his hand heavily on his shoulder and squeezed.

This was serious. Was it his dad's health? "What's going on?"

"This woman you brought home with you—"

"Alyson."

"Yes. What are your feelings toward this woman?"

His shoulders relaxed, and he breathed a sigh of relief. "Aw, Dad, come on." He rubbed his face. "We're just friends. Don't start planning a wedding just because I show up with a girl."

"And what are her feelings toward you?"

"I told you, we're just friends."

"Are you sure? You don't just step into a single mom's life only to step out of it again. If you aren't serious about this girl, this young mother, you shouldn't be leading her on like this."

"I'm not . . ." It shocked him how seriously his dad was taking this. "I'm not *leading her on*, Dad."

"You'd better make sure, son, because what I saw this morning didn't look like 'just friends.' She looks at you with pure devotion. And I don't see you returning that."

A zing coursed through him. "What? When was this?"

"You just want to be worshipped, is that it?" Lawrence butted in. "You need your adoring fans. Didn't you learn since the last girl you brought home?"

"Why are you bringing her into this? Yvonne has nothing to do with anything. And Alyson knows I teach school. She's not vain like that. Yvonne was a mistake." It was always the same—every single time he came home, someone had to bring up his failures.

His fiancé had been totally in love with him when she thought they were about to leave for Los Angeles. When she found out he had accepted a position in San Antonio as an elementary school teacher, she left him. Just like that. Said kids were never part of the bargain, and she knew what he really wanted, and it wasn't success.

"Just be careful, son. Being kind in the short run could be much crueler in the long run. Don't lead her on. A young mother is looking for a suitable *mate*, not a *friend*. Understand?"

All the men were quiet. He looked around the group, none of them met his gaze but Uncle Mason, who nodded. Even Uncle Mason thought he was in the wrong. The message sunk in. Whether or not he planned to, he was leading Alyson on just by being kind to her. A kindness that could turn cruel.

He'd just wanted to help her.

And—if he was totally honest with himself— maybe see if she was interested. He couldn't tell. He got glimpses sometimes—feelings, inklings, that maybe . . . but nothing concrete. Nothing to stand on. What had his dad seen?

"Lawrence, hand me the water, I've got to slow down these ribs."

The men started talking again, his dad and brother went back to paying attention to the meat and ignoring him. As usual. He walked away, dismissed and fuming. Nothing ever changed.

Chapter Nine

Alyson stepped out of the way as two more boys came yelling into the house then ran back out with cookies in hand. She took one last look out the back door at Andre playing happily in the sandbox with three other toddlers, watched over by two teen girls who took selfies, showed each other their screens and laughed.

"He'll be fine. Don't worry." Mama Dottie was suddenly at her side. "Selene and Bria are veteran babysitters. They seem like silly girls right now, but they do a good job."

"Do you need help with anything? I don't really know what to do with myself. I never have free time like this."

"I was just coming to fetch you. Come on to the kitchen. That's where we all get to catch up." Dottie waved for her to follow, and they entered the sunny yellow room with gleaming wood cabinets and an eight-seater wood-slab table where Marcus's grandmother had sat the night before.

Three women, two of them Marcus's sisters, sat at the table in chairs along the wall. The third—who she'd seen that morning when the kids were opening their presents—was smaller-boned, like

Alyson, and movie-star beautiful, with glossy hair almost to her waist, yet appeared perpetually unhappy. Alyson had yet to see the woman smile.

Food covered the granite countertops—cookie trays, popcorn balls and bags of chips, chopped vegetables waiting to be cooked, spices, herbs—the place was filled with color and so many scents. Chocolate and rosemary warred with each other for primacy. "You can help my girls shell pecans if you like." Dottie went back to preparing snap beans. "And if you're thirsty, help yourself. Glasses are in the cupboard next to the fridge."

She was thirsty and so got ice water from the three-door refrigerator—the same fridge she'd had in New York. Would she ever be able to afford nice things again? Calculations of tuition payments and daycare filled her mind, but she put it out with a shake of her head. She didn't need that anxiety bubbling up here. Like Marcus had said, she was on vacation.

She passed by the kitchen window and saw Marcus talking to his dad over a smoky grill. Marcus didn't look happy. Was he getting in trouble for surprising his family with uninvited guests?

"What are they grilling?"

"Bar-B-Q ribs. You like ribs?"

"Sure. Who doesn't?" Truthfully, she couldn't remember the last time she'd had ribs. Probably at a Chinese restaurant. She glanced at the table of women—Gail, she recognized, and she thought the other sister's name was Justine? The third woman was the one who had been glancing at her all morning like she was trying to figure her out.

To sit at the table with them, Alyson would have to pull the bench out from under the table and sit across from them and feel like she was being cross-examined by a panel of experts. Maybe she'd grab a snack instead. Stall the awkwardness. The biscuits that morning had been delicious, but as hungry as she was, she hadn't been able to eat much sitting so close to Marcus. She'd have to avoid being so near him from now on or she'd make a fool of herself. And starve.

She scanned the long counter for all the snacks to choose from and spied her cookies, sticking out like a sore thumb. Literally. The pale yellow of the shortbread squares and the pale pink of the cherry almond cookies looked like a sore thumb amidst the ooey-gooey chocolate cookies and brownies and bars topped with caramel and toasted coconut. She wished they were on the tray of kid-decorated, iced sugar cookies. They didn't really fit either tray. They, like her, just didn't fit anywhere.

"*Mere-mere* is napping." A middle-aged woman came in looking worn out. "Putting her meds in pudding worked like a charm." The woman—who looked old enough to be an aunt or young enough to be a sister—pulled out the bench with her foot and sat down.

"Thank you, Marianne." Dottie wiped her hands on a kitchen towel. "I still have a hard time of it when she gets like this. I miss my mama." The older woman teared up, but as Justine and Gail rallied around her, giving her hugs and touches of encouragement, she grew stronger. "I know it's a blessing to still have her with us. It just doesn't feel like it sometimes. I love her still. But, God, I miss her. I miss her so much."

Although the others were still hugging on and showing loving kindness to Mama Dottie, Marianne's gaze had zeroed in on Alyson.

Alyson looked down, suddenly feeling like a trespasser.

"Hi, I'm Marianne." She crossed the room to Alyson and offered her hand to shake. "You're . . .?"

"Alyson Daniels." She took Marianne's hand but felt her mistake as a pain slicing her heart. "Uh, Stefanelli." She rolled her eyes at herself. "Just Alyson. Nice to meet you."

"She's Marcus's girlfriend," Gail said casually, coming back to the table and digging in the bowl of pecans for another handful to crack.

"Um, actually—" Alyson tried.

"Isn't it illegal or something to date a student's parent?" Gail tapped the air with a pecan meat fork to emphasize her point.

"I . . . I don't know . . . and we're not . . ." Alyson tried again, now wondering if this could get Marcus in trouble if anyone at school found out. Darius couldn't keep a secret.

"How long have y'all been together?" said the beauty who'd been watching her.

"We're not really."

Justine smiled warmly. "He's never brought a girl home for Christmas before. I'm Justine, by the way. Sorry we bombarded you with names last night." She had a gentle voice and reminded Alyson of her own sweet-natured sister. Justine looked at the woman next to her expectantly, but she didn't introduce herself. "And Lana here is our brother Larry's wife."

Lana didn't bother to look up, ignoring social graces. What was her story?

"Yeah, he did too bring someone else home"—Gail poked the air with her utensil again—"it's just that he was already *engaged* before we ever got to meet her. Hmmph. I told him what I thought of *that*."

Marianne pulled the bench out farther so that Alyson could sit. Alyson was about to thank her when Marianne said, "You're not *engaged* are you?"

"No! Goodness, we're just friends. Honest."

"Just asking." Marianne ate one of the shelled pecans. "He's so darn secretive. We'd never know."

"That Yvonne girl just wasn't going to happen. She was *too much*. Even higher maintenance than me." Lana said. "He had his mid-life crisis a quarter-century ahead of schedule." Alyson sensed the woman was on her best behavior for the holiday gathering but could be mean.

"He didn't have an early mid-life crisis." Marianne rolled her eyes. "That girl was just taking advantage of him. He's too trusting."

"True. *So* true." Gail plucked pecan meat from the shell before turning her gaze on Alyson. "But bringing someone home for *Christmas*, you've got to be pretty serious already, right?"

"And the way your boys hang on him . . ." Lana's tone made it sound like a bad thing. "Y'all must've been together a long time?"

"All the kids love him. He's a kid magnet," Justine corrected her. "So how long *have* y'all been together?"

"Not long. I mean . . . we're not . . . together . . . officially." They weren't together at all, but she had no idea what he had told them, if anything. Was she supposed to keep up some sort of appearance for this weekend? Was *that* the reason he wanted her here?

She remembered that guilty look in the car when she'd mentioned correcting his mom's notion that she was his girlfriend. He hadn't bothered. She really needed to talk to him. She couldn't out-and-out *lie*, but she also didn't want to make things difficult for him.

"We're just friends. We're mostly here to trade out my Mercedes for a Toyota." She looked around at the disbelieving faces.

"No. I know my boy." His mom spoke up from the kitchen, now chopping pecans they had shelled. "This isn't about cars. It's never about *things* with him." She shook her head. "Just friends. Mmm-hhm."

Alyson took a deep breath and tried again. "I think he felt sorry for us because we were going to be alone for Christmas. And I didn't have a tree. He just felt sorry for us. That's all."

"Oh boy. We have it now." Marianne chuckled with a slow shake of the head, just like Marcus. Their mannerisms were so alike it was as if Marianne was just an older, female version of him.

"Yep, here it comes." Gail seemed almost giddy.

"What?" Alyson had no clue what they were talking about.

"He's a sucker for a sad story. Always has been. Stray puppies and kitties when he was a boy." Justine smiled fondly.

"Then befriending all the outcasts, nerds and weirdos in high school." Gail laughed.

"Not that you're a weirdo or anything." Justine corrected for Gail. "He's just a big softie."

"Well, he was one too. A band nerd. *Such* a nerd." Gail's smile couldn't get any bigger. "Wanna see?" She had a devilish gleam in her eyes. Hard to resist a look like that.

Gail disappeared down the hall a moment then came back with old family albums.

Alyson only half listened to his sisters as they rambled on about memories of places and times—details she'd never remember anyway—as they looked through the pictures. She saw him from when he was a baby all the way through high school.

Cute, chubby, happy baby. Cute, chubby, happy kid. Then the awkward stage when he was all arms and legs and uneven facial hair. Then he'd stopped smiling in the photos and started avoiding the camera. In half the candids of him, he was blocking the photo or trying to get out of frame.

Something had happened in high school to make him not just chubby like before, but fat. And unhappy. The only time he seemed happy in the photos was when he was holding an instrument. The photos of him stopped for a while, and then there was one, years later, Marcus slim and buff, with a modelesque woman on his arm. A female bodybuilder-type, with long blonde braids.

Alyson looked below the picture and saw it was a Save the Date card from three years ago. She suddenly felt like a sack of potatoes. She could never compare to that kind of beauty. It was like comparing her pasty, lumpy old self to Beyoncé.

Stop it, Alyson. She closed her eyes. The conversation with his sisters was getting to her. Of course he wasn't attracted to her. Why would she even think so? They were only colleagues. He was just overly nice, trying to be helpful. *Get a grip!*

Lana pointed to a photo. "I didn't know he played clarinet, too. Is there an instrument he *doesn't* play?"

"I bet he's never played the bagpipes," Alyson offered. She tried to infuse her voice with some pep but seeing that Save the Date card had turned her mood dark. She had looked just as happy in her newlywed pictures and look where that had ended up. What was the point?

At least seeing who he was attracted to took some of the pressure off, and she could stop being so nervous around him. There was no possible way he could feel the same about her as she did about him. She was a lump of coal in the bottom of an unclaimed stocking.

"No. No bagpipes, but he'd figure 'em out," Dottie said, clearly listening to every word. "He's just like his gramps. My daddy. Jazz musician his whole life. Every instrument was just an extension of the man, not a separate thing."

Gail shoved the album out of the way and slid some cracked pecans to her, so Alyson added her hands to the work. The album was still open to the Save the Date card, Marcus smiling joyfully, full of hope. What had happened to destroy that hope?

Justine and Lana still leafed through the other album. Lana smiled now, looking at the past. So it was just the present that made her unhappy.

"Did your father sing, too? Marcus has an amazing voice." The last was out before she realized it. She hadn't meant to lead the conversation there.

"He did." Something in Dottie's tone had Alyson meeting her gaze. Dottie wiped her hands on a mistletoe kitchen towel and stepped closer. "You've heard Marcus sing?"

"Yes, that's ..." Alyson stopped herself from giving away how they had met and what he had done for her at the mall. She was so horrible at lying. It was the one thing he didn't want her to talk about, so of course it was at the top of her mind.

"Did you see his band?" Marianne said. "I've never seen them play."

She hesitated then let out a heavy sigh. He may hate her for this, but he shouldn't be hiding from his family. "Here." She dug her phone out of her back pocket. "He's got his own YouTube channel. And he's on Facebook Live every week." She found his station easily—she had bookmarked it. She tapped Play, and a video of Marcus playing classical guitar started, the screen filled with fingers on strings, no face shots. "This one's my favorite. He's pretty amazing." She handed the phone to his sisters who gobbled it up.

"What? He changed his name!" Gail tucked her chin into her neck in outrage, her face drawn in tight. Now she was the one who looked like a sore thumb.

Alyson couldn't suppress her smile. "Lots of entertainers do that. It protects their privacy, their families."

"Have you seen this, Mama?" Marianne held it so her mom could see it better. The video ended, and Dottie tentatively touched the phone, to start it playing again.

"He never shares his music with me, anymore. Not since high school. It's *beautiful*." Her voice carried a profound woundedness and surprise at his obvious talent.

"He didn't exactly share it with me, either. But I put two and two together and went hunting. You should check out the saxophone video if you really want to be wowed. But don't tell him I told you." She took the phone back and scrolled for Dottie's sake, who seemed uncomfortable navigating.

"Girl, you're a little stalker." Gail smiled and nodded her appreciation of the fact. "Look at you, all sneaky-sneaky."

"Where's his singing?" Dottie asked. "He won't do solos at the church anymore. It's all we can do to get him to sing with the choir on holidays."

"Oh, um, his channel doesn't have those videos." Oh boy. She was getting herself into a mess—if they went searching for those videos, they would find Marcus's Elf Caroling videos, and he'd be super mad at her for telling them.

"How did you hear him then?" Marianne cocked her head to the side.

Maybe a partial truth? "Um, well, I was in charge of the Winter Wonderland at the mall where I work, and I was having a horrible day—everything was going wrong, and the crowd was getting angry. And Marcus stepped up and entertained the crowd for me by singing Christmas carols and telling stories. He was amazing. Saved the day, and probably my job."

"He does like to save a damsel in distress." A dry comment from Gail.

"Gail," Mama Dottie warned.

"What? It's true. He wants to save everyone, and then they end up dropping him like a ton of bricks. He has *horrible* luck. Everyone takes advantage of the poor guy."

"Gail!"

"What?" Gail followed Dottie's glance toward Alyson. "Oh. Well, I don't mean *you*."

Alyson laughed and continued the intricate work of shelling a broken pecan, the phone still softly playing Marcus's music. "It's okay. He's made it *very clear* that we're just friends."

"How rude! He said that?" Justine piped up, brow furrowed.

"No, no, it's not rude. It's honest. I mean, he's got things he wants to do with his life." She changed tools, using the needle edge to pull out the stubborn pecan meat. "He'll be moving to L.A. someday. And, well, friends is all I can handle." She poked the meat in the shell and pulled, but it wouldn't budge. She scowled at the stupid nut. "As soon as school starts, I'm sure we'll both go back to our usual routines."

Silence caused her to look up. She realized everyone had taken what she'd said all wrong. Gail pressed her lips, her eyes narrowed, Lana shook her head, and Justine frowned with pity, her hand over her heart. Marianne looked at her with some curiosity, cocking her head even further than before. Alyson glanced at Mama Dottie, but she walked back to where she was chopping the pecans, the bowl of freshly shelled ones in her hand. She seemed somehow sad. What had she said to upset everyone?

"My brother, the rake," Gail muttered. "Mama, do we have enough pecans yet?"

"Keep shelling. I'll give you the bowl back in a sec. We've got New Year's potluck at the church, you know."

"So how did you meet?" Lana asked. "The school? Like a parent-teacher conference type thing?"

"Well, he is Darius's favorite teacher, but—"

"So you've been seeing each other since September, and he didn't tell us? That dog." Gail grimaced as a pecan she cracked shattered.

"Ladies," Mama Dottie interrupted. "Didn't you hear her say they're not an item? Leave the poor girl alone. Let her breathe."

The silence lasted only a few seconds before Dottie walked the now-empty bowl back to the table for them and stopped to pat Alyson's shoulder. "So then, what's *your* story, Alyson dear? Why were you alone this Christmas?" All eyes glanced her way, but they didn't pressure her with continued stares.

How much to tell? She sighed. "I'm recently divorced." The words felt both alien and somehow stale on her lips. Like she'd said it a thousand times already, but couldn't quite convince herself it was true. "You probably guessed that by now."

"How recent?" Justine covered Alyson's hand with her own.

"Hey." Gail leaned on the table. "I'm *still* fighting with *my* ex, two years later. What did your idiot XY do?" Gail seemed eager to fight for her. Alyson loved her for it and loved Justine's immediate sympathy. Her heart swelled, and her eyes began to fill, so she pulled back and took another deep breath.

Alyson hadn't had anyone to talk to for so long, unable to confide in her employees, unable to cry to her mom without getting an earful of 'you should have done this, you should have done that.'

It was exhilarating and scary, and the back of her neck broke out in a thin sweat as she realized she was about to tell complete strangers her truth and shame.

Chapter Ten

Alyson examined the shiny metal pecan fork as she rolled it between finger and thumb. Telling her story would mean reliving it. Was she strong enough? Was it time?

"This past July, the boys and I went on vacation to the shore like usual—Montauk, Long Island. We lived in Manhattan. *Every* July since we moved there, we had a family vacation. But this time, Will, my ex, didn't show, kept stalling. Vacation was almost over, but we'd been rocky since I got pregnant with Andre, and Will always was a workaholic, so I didn't think much of it." She blew out the rest of her breath in a huff and set down the pecan fork. "But then my mom calls, yelling about how I've ruined her open house and she's going to have to put off the sale of her home now, and what in the world was I thinking sending a moving pod of my stuff to her home?"

Sharp intake of breath. "He didn't." This from Justine who once again held her hand at her heart.

Gail shook her head, looking hard.

Alyson nodded. "He did. On our way back from the shore, I find that my credit cards don't work anymore. We get home and find he'd done us the *favor* of moving us out. All of my stuff and the boys' stuff went to my mother's and all the rest of our things, our furniture in common, was all gone. The apartment in Manhattan we were subletting was returning to its owner. Will was going to be on site in D.C. for his law firm, and I was to go home to Texas. I was served with divorce papers right then and there."

"You never saw it coming." Marianne's voice was low and soft, not at all blaming.

"No. I mean, we'd been having trouble, but nothing I thought warranted divorce. But he'd obviously been planning it a long time. As soon as he landed his dream job, we started seeing less and less of him, and frankly, I didn't *want* to see him. I haven't missed him." She crossed her arms in a self-hug. It had been so hard, so scary, to start over.

"When we married, he'd wanted to change the world, and I was going to change it right along with him. But by the time he got where he wanted to be, it was all about making money and living the high life. *Family not included.* Once I was heavy with Andre, we lived separate lives." Alyson shrugged, suffering a million tiny memories of fights and worries and knowing he was on something, knowing he was hiding something from her, never able to reach him, a million memories pelting her like sleet on her bare face.

"Is the court dragging its feet on the child support?" Gail was the first to break the silence. She cracked a nut with renewed fervor. "That's what happened to me. Three payments behind since the beginning, and he's always trying to get the payments lowered."

"No. There is no child support. That's my fault." She took the pecan pick in hand and turned it over in her fingers again, examining not it, but the ugly past. "He gave me two options—custody battle where he would likely win, since I had no means to support myself yet or, I get the kids without a battle but forgo child support. I panicked. I signed. And he knew I would. He knew I would do anything to make sure my babies stayed with me. But he made it *my* choice. So he could go with a clear conscience."

"Heavens!" Dottie came and stood beside her. "You mean he gave up his own sons, his flesh and blood, just so he wouldn't have to pay for them?"

"Why that rotten—" Marianne started.

"It wasn't about money. It was about winning. It was about freedom. We were a dead weight to him, dragging him down. So he cut us free." Deep cleansing breath. It felt good to say it all out loud and know people were actually listening, really hearing what she was saying instead of telling her what she'd done wrong.

"Alyson," Dottie said, squeezing her shoulder, "hold on to that word, 'free.' Because that's exactly what you are. Jesus took you out of that situation to give you a second chance when your husband went astray of the Lord. And don't you let anybody tell you different. God's got plans for you. Plans with a capital P."

Gail rolled her tearful eyes and laughed. "Oh, Mom, don't go full-Jesus on her yet, you'll scare her away."

Justine and Marianne both chuckled. It seemed to be a private joke.

The back door flew open, and Darius came running. "Mom! Mom! Mom! You gotta come play! We need you on our team!"

Marcus came in behind him, and the mood of the room seemed to hit them both at the same time. Their smiles dropped like stones. "Hey, little man, let your mom talk to the grown-ups for a while, all right? Let's go back outside." Marcus touched his shoulder to guide him back out, but Darius charged forward to his mom.

"What's wrong, Mommy? Why are you crying?"

Alyson wiped her cheeks. She hadn't even felt the tears roll, but sure enough, her cheeks were wet.

She looked up to see Marcus glancing around at all of them in turn. Alyson snatched her phone from the middle of the table, turning off the quiet replay of his music, hoping he hadn't heard it. But he tracked the motion with his gaze and did a double take when he saw the photo albums on the table, one of them still open to dorky fat pictures of a past Christmas. The other album was open to the Save the Date postcard where he'd looked so happy holding on to that modelesque woman.

He crossed the room and snapped both of the albums shut.

"Why?" He narrowed his gaze at Gail.

"Oh, relax, Marcus, we were just having fun."

"Go on back outside, please, Darius." His voice was gentle and firm as he looked at her son. Darius obeyed with just a wave to her before he took off. She wasn't sure how she felt about that. She'd been usurped.

"If I wanted her to see these things, I'd have shown her myself." He stacked the photo albums and moved them to the edge of the table. She got the idea he was deliberately avoiding her gaze. He started to follow Darius back outside.

"Why would you care if a *friend* saw these pics?" Gail chased after him. "Not just a friend, then, is she?"

He turned on her. "Shutup, Gail. You don't know what you're talking about." Then a glance back at Alyson. "Did you make her cry, Gail? Poking and poking at whatever hurts until someone comes undone?"

Alyson saw Dottie's concern for her son raise a notch in the way her worried gaze followed him.

"Why are you getting all het up about a bunch of silly photos?" Lana's voice was unnecessarily defensive, as if he accused her.

"It's not about the photos." He spoke calmly now. "And you wonder why I never come home anymore? Everybody in this house just wants to live in the past. Poke fun at my failures every time I come home. I can't ever become who I want to be. Not here."

"Stop overreacting, Marcus," Marianne said. "You're acting a fool in front of your . . . Alyson."

He looked from Marianne to Gail to his mom and back to Marianne, never once meeting Alyson's gaze though she wanted him to. She wanted him to know she didn't think of him any differently. That *failure* was not a word she equated with him at all.

"Unbelievable." He shook his head. He walked out, and they heard the front door open and close.

Alyson got up to follow him.

"You should let him cool off. He'll be okay," Gail warned her.

"Yes, that will only make him retreat more." Dottie wore a long frown and Alyson knew she felt like she was losing her son. The worry plain on her face said this was not just about some photos. This ran deep. Alyson had never seen her gentle giant so upset before.

"Good thing I don't know him as well as you guys do." She stood and brushed the pecan skins from her hands. "That gives me a good excuse." She saluted the surprised women and followed him out the door.

By the time Alyson caught up to him, he was shooting hoops in the driveway. He had a sour look on his face—not mad, not sad, sour.

"Don't you think you're being a little tough on your mom?"

"Yeah? How so?" He didn't look at her but took another shot, his flat tone clearly indicating he didn't care what she thought.

"You arrive at her house on Christmas Eve with a strange woman and two kids you didn't tell her about, and you expect them not to overreact by thinking I'm your girlfriend? I warned you." She stood akimbo, making herself as big as she could. He *would* notice her, look at her.

"And they weren't being ugly about anything. They didn't mean to hurt you. They were just being nice to me, to make me feel part of the group. It's not their fault I cried. I cry a lot these days. It's annoying, but I can't help it."

He missed his shot, the ball rebounding toward her. She caught it and held on to it, waiting for him to talk to her. He still wouldn't look at her, just held out his hand for the ball.

"Nope. My ball." She dribbled the ball in place, hoping to draw him out. She had wondered why he'd been eager to help her and had figured it was because of Darius and wanting to give him a good Christmas. But a new idea had just occurred to her. A more selfish, and thus more likely, reason for him to want them along this weekend. "I think you brought us home with you because you *don't* want them to ask you about your life. We're just a big deflector for you, aren't we? A distraction."

Taking a moment to focus on her form, she took the quick step-step-jump for a perfect lay-up. *Swoosh!* "Two points to team Stefanelli," she mimicked a sports announcer's voice and tossed him the ball.

It had the desired effect—he finally met her gaze. "All they've got is the past because you won't share your present. If you want the dynamic to change, change it." She crouched in the ready position. "Well? It's your ball, come on."

"Are we really doing this?" He pointed from the ball to the hoop. His sour look demolished by a tentative grin.

"Only if you feel comfortable losing to a girl." She deepened her crouch, ready to spring.

"Oooh! Man! You are pretty *fierce* for a half-pint."

She smacked the ball from his hands, dribbled and took the shot, rebounded and took another before he'd even woken up. *Swoosh!*

"Four and ZEEEROOO. Better get in the game." She chest-passed him the ball, hard.

"Did you play—"

"In high school, yeah. They called me the badger. 'Cause I'm little, but I'm mean." She crouched again, ready. "Come on, big guy, give me all you got. I'll bite your kneecaps off."

His eyebrows arched in surprise, then he laughed and laughed, which was just what she'd been going for. It was such a fun, joyful sound she couldn't help but giggle too. Movement at the kitchen window caught her eye. His sisters watched in amazement. She waved, and all left the window but Gail, who gave Alyson a thumb's up.

‰⁊

Still smiling, Marcus dribbled the ball a few times. Alyson sure was something else. He watched her match his weaving stance, her bright eyes looking up at him. Eager to play. Happy she'd made him laugh. Those eyes widened the hollowness in his heart.

Maybe he hadn't been totally honest with himself. Maybe Alyson was right—it wasn't about him helping her get back on her feet or mend her wounded heart, maybe it was about him using them as a shield, giving people something to talk about rather than pressuring him to move back home and work for the church. It hadn't even occurred to him until she'd said it. Then again, until his dad said it, it also hadn't occurred to him that he might be misleading Alyson, that he might hurt her. He should have taken the bus and not gotten involved. But those eyes . . .

"We can't play as long as you keep frowning like that." She walked away from him, then leaned against the minivan a few yards down the long driveway. "Come tell me what's going on with you. Then we'll finish the game."

Even as he walked toward her, he doubted he could say anything at all. He wasn't even sure why he followed, except that it was nice to have someone's undivided attention for a change.

"So, was it that argument with your dad that set you off? I saw you through the window."

"You saw that?" A queasy feeling overtook him for just a second until he reasoned she'd seen it, but not heard it. "Yeah, it made me mad. I haven't seen

him since July and the first thing he says to me is—
" He looked at her, leaning against the hood of the vehicle, head propped on her hand, open and waiting. Beautiful. He took a deep breath. "Well, it doesn't matter what he said. The point is he yelled at me for nothing and never asked me how I'm doing or what I'm doing. He just assumes I'm going to fail."

"He said that?"

"No. But he doesn't have to. He thinks I'm a joke. Always has. He's never taken me seriously." He hadn't meant to say that out loud and glanced her way to gauge her reaction.

"Could you be projecting your own fears on him?"

He glowered, but she responded by reaching out and touching his arm. Not what he expected. It took the heat from his anger.

"He's the one you tried to please when you were growing up, isn't he?"

He didn't say anything. Couldn't say anything. What she said made sense and brought forth memories of past failures with his dad, of never being seen unless he screwed up somehow. Failure and shame, a never-ending cycle.

"For me, it was my mom. Couldn't ever quite please her. And I'm still doing it to myself. Whenever I feel like a failure, I hear it in my mom's voice, but I *know* she loves me. I *know* she wants what's best for me. Even if she can't say it without nagging. Maybe it's the same with your dad."

"Yeah. Maybe." He *did* know his dad loved him. He just had a rotten way of showing it. Always pushing working for the church as if Marcus needed a safety net. As if he couldn't achieve his goals.

"What did you fight about this time?"

"Nothing." He never was a good liar.

Her raised eyebrow called him on it. She took the ball from him. "Oh. That means it was about me. About us. I knew we shouldn't have come." She dribbled and shot. It rebounded, and he caught it.

"The fault was mine, not yours. He thinks . . ." He couldn't tell her his dad thought he was leading her on.

"He thinks there's more going on between us than there is?"

"Yeah. I couldn't set him straight. And if there's *not* anything going on between us, then I'm *still* wrong."

"Your mom and sisters were the same. It was kind of weird, but here's the takeaway: They all want you to be happy, and they don't think you are."

He cocked his head. Why would they think he was unhappy? "What did you tell them?"

"That we're just friends. That we haven't known each other that long. But I'm not sure I got through to anyone but your mom. You should talk to her. That 'not coming home' comment made her sad. She didn't deserve that." Alyson put her hands out for the ball, and he tossed it to her. She took the shot and scored. "Six to zero."

"Come on! We're not really playing."

"Said like someone sore at looooosiiing." She sang the last and held the ball out to him again. "No? All right. Make it and take it." She dribbled, shot and scored again. "Eight to zero. Badger over Giant Elf."

"Oh, that's it." He stepped forward. "Gimme that ball."

She handed it over with a smile, but the first step he took, she tried to slap it out of his hands. He made to shoot, but she yelled out so fast it was one blurred word: "Gotta-dribble-before-you-shoot-or-it-doesn't-count."

"You took two turns!" He tried dribbling behind him and almost lost the ball to a scary quick demon in heels he'd had no idea was so competitive. "You're crazy, woman!" He towered over her, but it didn't stop her from jumping in front of him and waving her arms, getting in his face. He shot and scored.

"My ball!" She sang, skipping after it, her thick red hair swinging across her back. He liked this version of her. This playful side. She scooped up the ball and dribbled back to the far side of the driveway from the hoop, playing more by the rules now than they had been. He half-heartedly raised his arms to block her, and she pounded him in the chest with the ball. "Ow!"

"You'd better take me seriously!"

He guarded for real now, towering over her, there was no way she could get off a shot. She bent backward and dribbled behind her. The girl had skills for sure. He started to straighten to watch her work but she goaded him, "Don't you want the ball? Eight-two is so sad."

He bent forward, behind her to shake the ball from her, but quickly found the closeness, the intimacy, was too much—almost an embrace.

She smiled. "You so want to foul right now, don't you?"

That was *exactly* what he wanted. Now who was leading on whom?

"No holding." She dipped into a squat and sprang up his left flank, then performed a perfect layup. "Ten-two, Badger on top. I think we should stop now, this is getting embarrassing for you."

He grabbed her and threw her over his shoulder, her squealing laughter his reward. He called out in referee voice, "Holding on Giant Elf!" Then he dribbled the ball she dropped. One handed, he shot and scored.

"My ball! My ball!" She squirmed toward where the ball had bounced off and nearly slipped over his shoulder head-first onto the pavement. He secured her more firmly against him, suddenly aware his hands held the backs of her warm thighs, his cheek grazed her denim-clad hip. He needed to end this, or he'd embarrass himself for sure.

"Stop wiggling, I'll let you down."

"I'll shoot from here. I want a slam dunk. Get me the ball."

He chuckled at her authoritative tone even when hanging upside down over his shoulder. "Yes, ma'am."

He lined up where the ball was, then kneeled so she could pick it up.

"Okay, hold me tight."

"I've got you." He tightened his grip as she straightened herself, now upright. Her knees dug into his ribs, but he didn't care. He only hoped she couldn't feel how fast his heart was beating holding her against himself like this. She wobbled in his grasp, but he didn't dare put a hand on her bottom to steady her. A week ago, she'd been untouchable. Now he never wanted to let her go.

"Closer. A little closer."

He stepped backward.

"To the left. Sorry—my left, your right. There!" She raised up and slammed the ball through the hoop, hanging on it for just a second.

He felt her lift an inch before settling back against him.

"Woohoo! Slam DUNK!" She raised her arms in victory and leaned back so much that he had no choice but to steady her.

He released her enough to let her slide down his body, only thinking a second later that wasn't helping his condition at all. He couldn't let go, he could only stare into her beaming smile. A smile that unraveled him.

"I'm next! I wanna slam dunk!"

Marcus jumped at the voices. Darius and Moses ran toward them. His mom called out from the front door, "You boys get back here, it's time to eat!" The boys went charging back toward the house. Then his mom gave him a long look, one he couldn't read, and went back inside.

"You should probably let go of me now."

He held her around the waist, her sweater bunched up beneath his hand. He pulled back like she was fire itself. "Sorry."

No wonder his mom had looked at him so funny.

Chapter Eleven

Alyson felt Marcus's hand at her back as he ushered her through the doorway. Such a simple thing, but even that innocent touch made her tingle. All eyes were on them as they entered the kitchen but soon returned to a bustling exodus of food heading outside for the barbeque while the sun was still strong enough to warm them.

"Marcus, honey, would you take this, please?" His mom held out a casserole dish of baked beans.

He took the dish from her and kissed her cheek. "Thank you, Mama." He spun around with the beans then kissed her other cheek.

"What on earth!" She laughed at his antics. "Whatever for?"

"For being gracious and kind and joyful my whole life. Sorry I acted like a child." He kissed her once more on the forehead and then walked away. "Darius, grab those rolls and come on outside. Time to eat!"

Darius grabbed the basket of rolls, but instead of following Marcus out directly, he came to Alyson and waved her down to his level. Then he planted a big wet kiss on her forehead. "Thanks, Mom!" He laughed triumphantly and ran to catch up to Marcus.

Dottie laughed. "Well, isn't he just the cutest little mimic?"

Alyson touched both hands to her heart. "I'm so glad he has someone like Marcus to learn from. Better a caring teacher than a neglectful father." Thank God for Marcus so her son could learn how to be a man even without his father around. She said a silent prayer of thanks that he *wasn't* learning from his father.

Gail handed her a pot of green beans with bacon, and she carried it out to the feast, feeling like she was part of it all.

After Marcus's brother said a quick grace over the barbeque, everyone gathered around the buffet table and loaded their plates. Family, friends, and neighbors settled along four picnic tables and overflowed to folding chairs, Dottie and Gail opting for just walking around chatting with everyone.

"Over here, Darius!" Alyson tracked the voice and saw Darius's friend Moses along with his siblings and mother, Marianne.

Marianne poked her oldest boy and pointed toward the buffet. "Joe, go make your daddy a plate before all the ribs are gone." Joe, in the pimply awkward stage, left straightaway.

"Big Joe's working today?" Marcus asked. "I thought he'd be here since he worked yesterday."

"On call. Got called in." For Alyson, Marianne added, "ER nurse. Both of us are." Moses scooted down the bench, making room for them. Darius sat next to Moses.

Marcus surprised her by lightly steadying her at the elbow as she stepped over the bench to sit. Why was he suddenly treating her like she was fragile?

"We want to play b-ball with you guys after lunch, okay, Mom?" Darius bounced in his seat. "Okay?"

"We'll see. The sun goes down so early. I want you to finish that plate, okay?"

"Aww, Mom. It'll be dark by the time I finish this."

"Better get started then."

"Who won?" Moses asked, his mouth already smeared with barbeque sauce.

"I did," they answered in unison.

She elbowed Marcus in the ribs playfully.

"She outscored me, but I won." Marcus sounded proud.

"That's not possible." Moses pointed a half-eaten rib at him.

"It is when it's a *contact* sport." Marianne raised an eyebrow to them both. "Eat your ribs, child, don't point with them," she admonished her son.

Alyson grinned and tried to catch Marcus's eye, but he'd taken Marianne's comment more seriously than she had and wasn't smiling anymore. There had to be something else bothering him. She'd get to the bottom of it, eventually.

Instead, she focused on trying to get some macaroni and cheese and green beans into Andre, which was difficult because he wanted to build with the green beans, stacking them in orderly piles. She listened to the conversations swirling around her, listened to Marcus chat with Marianne about her crazy-busy job.

A cold wind blew in, shaking the leaves from the trees. One landed right on her plate. Conversation ceased for a moment, and then several people announced what they were all thinking: "Cold front's here!" The wind gusted through again as if in call and response.

"Grandpa, can we have a fire tonight?" One of the teen girls who'd babysat Andre earlier looked at her grandfather big pleading eyes.

"If it drops like they said on the TV."

Excitement swept through the younger crowd, who abandoned their food as they started playing again and talking about fires and s'mores. Marianne left to cover the food dishes, protecting them from falling leaves.

Alyson laughed at how Andre licked the barbeque sauce off the rib rather than take a bite. The wind blew right through her thin sweater, and she shivered, pulling her arms close to her body.

"You cold?" Marcus rose from his seat and came around to her other side, blocking the wind, and sitting so close she could feel his heat. He straddled the bench and watched her feed Andre.

She glanced at him from time to time, but he seemed content just to watch. She knew from the heat in her cheeks she was blushing, and for no reason but his closeness. The intensity of sitting alone with him in silence was almost more than she could bear. How did he keep doing that to her? Did he know? Could he feel it too?

"Let me." He held out his hands for Andre and while holding him around his middle, took the rib and took a healthy bite, playing up how he ripped the meat from the bone, as the ribs were so tender no tearing was necessary.

Andre laughed and tried taking a bite with his little teeth—and the rest of the meat slid right off the bone, hanging from his mouth. Poor Andre's eyes went huge with a silent "Uh-oh!" Alyson and Marcus couldn't help but laugh. Smiling, Andre let the meat fall.

Another gust of wind and Marcus leaned in, adding his warm hand to her back, Andre between them. She felt his hand stiffen then leave. Seeking why, she looked up in time to see a disapproving look from Marcus's dad, replaced by a small smile as he walked inside.

"I don't think your dad likes me very much."

"That's not true. Everybody likes you. It's something between me and him."

Clouds blocked the warmth of the sun.

She was pretty sure what was coming between Marcus and his father was *her*.

Andre leaned into her and put his head down. Barbeque sauce all over her sweater. "Are you ready for a nap, my love?" He snuggled under her chin. "No," came his sleepy, muffled reply.

She smiled up at Marcus, hoping he caught the humor, but he had a mix of emotions on his face, none of them humorous in the least. He saw her and smiled, obviously covering. "You want to go inside?"

He helped her from the picnic table with the gentle seriousness of a man dealing with a pregnant woman made of eggshells and explosives. Why was he suddenly so attentive? What had happened to the laughing man who'd thrown her over his shoulder?

She had a feeling, based on his dad's reproachful look, there would be no more fun between them. She had a feeling, whatever his reason for having her meet his family, she'd somehow already failed some sort of test. She had a feeling they were over before they'd even had a chance to begin.

༄༅

"Thanks for helping clean up some, Alyson." Dottie wiped her hands on a hand towel hanging near the kitchen sink. "You'd better get a paper towel, dear, this one's soppin' wet."

Alyson did as instructed. "You're welcome. Happy to help." She wiped up bits of water here and there on the counter before tossing the paper towel in the trash. She caught Dottie smiling at her. "You know, it took Lana two years before she offered to clean my kitchen with me."

"Mama, you're not being fair," Marianne spoke up from the long wooden table where she sat with their grandmother making sure she took her evening pills. "Lana was a twenty-year-old socialite when she married Larry and didn't know nothing about nothing. Doing dishes was out of her purview, Mama. Not her fault."

"Well, anyway, thank you for volunteering, dear. Little things mean a lot." Dottie patted her shoulder with her warm, soft hand.

Gail appeared in the doorway, leaning in sideways. "Y'all coming? Fire's going. Charades are starting."

"If it's all right with you guys," Alyson said, "I'd like to hang back and make a call. Wish my mom a merry Christmas."

Dottie smiled a closed-lip smile that contained such love. "Of course, dear. Tell your mama we just love having you and the boys and wish her a very merry Christmas from us too."

"And now we'll get out of your hair." Gail took her mom's arm and began to usher her away, but Dottie hesitated and said, "Why don't you go on and have some fun, Marianne. I'll watch over *Maman.*"

"No. You take care of her day in and day out. You go take a break."

"The nurse has spoken." Gail nodded to her mom and successfully ushered her out of the room this time. Marianne stayed with the now-dozing grandmother.

"Do you think your mom would mind if I made a pot of tea? I should have asked while she was still here."

Instead of answering, Marianne came into the kitchen and pulled down the kettle and a glazed earthenware teapot. "Here you go. Wasn't sure how to tell you where they were. She won't mind, especially if you make a full pot so she can have some."

Marianne sat near her grandmother again but moved her chair so she could better hear what was going on in the great room. Lots of faraway laughter and a familiar voice squealing "Oh no! I don't know how to do this one!"

"Justine. Bless her heart. She can't do improv to save her life. Got the best grades out of all of us, but when the pressure's on, she's a total airhead." Marianne laughed to herself, her face filled with affection for her sister.

"If you want to go join them, I'll watch over her. I'll yell for you when she wakes up."

Marianne cocked her head. "Really? You'd do that?"

"Sure. I'll just be making tea and calling my mom. Maybe she'll sleep through it all."

Marianne was halfway out of the room as she said, "I owe you one! Be back in a flash."

Once the water was on to boil, she dialed her mom, using the Bluetooth earpiece so her hands were free to measure out the loose-leaf tea she'd brought from home.

The call connected. "Hey, sweetie! Oh how I wish you were here! We're having a ball! Baby Angelica. She's just so precious. Perfect as a doll. Has her daddy's curly hair. Well, of course you've seen the pictures, but they just don't do her justice. She's just like you when you were a baby—curious about everything, not content to sit still. And guess what they surprised me with?"

"Hi, Mom. Wow." She hadn't heard her mom so animated in years.

"Guess!"

"I have no idea. Not a clue." Amy's husband was loaded, a fourth-generation olive oil industry tycoon. It could be anything.

"They've built me a mother-in-law cottage behind their house! I have a 1/1 in the same hacienda style as the main house. It's so cute! It's got a tiny little kitchen and a reading nook. I'm getting my deposit back from the retirement condo just as soon as they open on Monday."

Alyson's breath caught in her throat. Her mother wasn't coming home again. Why would she? "That's great, Mom. I'm so happy for you."

"Yes, and I can be here for little Angelica. Poor Amy is still so tired. This delivery almost killed her, they said. Why didn't they tell us that? And she can't have another one. It's too dangerous. She's beside herself. *Just beside herself.*"

"Sorry we spoiled your plans, Mom. You should've been there months ago, I know. I'm sorry."

It was a moment before her mother responded, curtly, no longer animated. "Nonsense, dear. Don't blame yourself. Amy's fine, the baby's fine. Everything worked out the way it needed to."

The kettle whistled. She hurried to remove it so as not to wake the old woman.

"What's that, sweetheart?"

"I'm making tea." She poured the steaming water into the pot, the loose leaves of Earl Grey swimming around like mermaids. "I brought the traditional cookies, too, so maybe we can still have tea and cookies together." Her voice sounded a little too chipper, but she was trying to hide the fact it bugged her that her mom was having such a great time away from her and hadn't bothered to ask about her or the boys.

"Oh, Alyson, I'm sorry, sweetie, I wish you'd called sooner, we're about to go to the city for Christmas dinner at some resort called Veladora. It's Paolo's family's tradition. You know, when in Rome . . ."

"Yes, Mom, I get it. I'll let you go. It's way past tea time here anyway."

"Oh, don't sound so glum, you old sourpuss. Everything is looking up. Just think. Now I have this mother-in-law cottage, selling the house isn't such an emergency. Since I won't need as much for my retirement as I thought, I can even split some of the house money with you for managing the sale and help you get a fresh start. See? It's looking up, up, up."

A fresh start. Right. The one blessing out of her horrible divorce was that she'd had her mom to come home to, to share bills with, and to help with the boys. Now it would all be up to her. Every last little detail. It exhausted her to even think about it. And it hadn't escaped her that her mother expected her to manage the sale of the house in her absence. So she really wasn't coming back, then?

"Thanks, Mom. Will you be coming home in January?"

"Let's talk about this later, sweetheart. We're about to leave now. Everyone, say Merry Christmas to Alyson!"

In sing-song voices, a mixed crowd of males and females chorused "Merry Christmas" over the phone, and one deep voice added "*Feliz Navidad.*" Her mother's laughter. "Oh, Richard, you always have to be the different one." Was her mother *flirting* with someone?

She disconnected the call, not waiting for her mom's customary "bye-bye for now" and took off the stupid Bluetooth device. Such an idiot. She'd sounded like a sentimental fool with her pathetic tea and cookies. Her mom had never offered to come stay with *her* when she'd had Darius or

Andre. And now she was leaving when Alyson needed her most.

Alyson leaned on the counter, her hands covering her face, and sobbed.

"Is the tea ready? I take mine with cream. Please and thank you."

Alyson stood straight, surprised, her tears forgotten. Marcus's grandmother was awake and wanted tea. Should she yell for Marianne? She heard another volley of laughter. "Okay, okay. Get this, y'all. This is a good one." Oh dear. It sounded like Marianne might actually be the one performing.

She wiped the tears from her cheeks and busied herself with finding cups and saucers, spoons, everything she needed.

"Don't let it get cold now. What kind is it? Smells familiar. Smells like Edinburgh."

Chapter Twelve

Alyson stopped in her tracks on the way to the table, the tea cups jostling on the saucers. "You've been to Edinburgh, Scotland?"

"Oh, child, I've been everywhere." She opened her arms wide. And let them drop. "But I haven't been on a plane in I don't know how long. I'm grounded. Stuck here till I die, I reckon. Hand me one of them shortbreads, I love shortbread."

Alyson did as she was told, wondering for a second if Marianne and Dottie would approve. But Marianne had given her the pills in pudding, so maybe sugar wasn't an issue.

The old woman ate the cookie, crumbs falling to her chest. "Buttery goodness. Yes, yes, just like I remember. Those were great years. Me and my Milton. All over Britain and France. So few colored Americans traveled abroad in the 50s that we were a sensation everywhere we went. And when they heard him play . . . Like angels tapping on your very heart. He wanted you to cry, you'd be nothing but tears. He wanted you happy, he'd play a little ditty that you'd hum and whistle for days after. Everybody loved my Milton."

The woman's proud face turned melancholy, her lips quivering. Alyson didn't want her to cry. How would she explain that to the others? "Miss, um, Missus . . ." She realized she didn't know her last name.

"Yes, child? Oh, is my tea ready?"

"Yes, ma'am. Just a moment." She poured the Earl Grey slowly, added a button of cream, and carefully stirred. Grandmother seemed content to watch the process. Alyson handed her the tea cup, careful to stay with her in case it was too much or too small to hold. She needn't have worried. Grandmother held it with both hands, fully realizing her limitations, and sipped gracefully.

Alyson did the math in her head. Marcus's brother was twelve years older than him, making him forty, so Dottie was likely in her early sixties, and that put Grandmother in her early to mid-eighties. At least. Wow. She didn't know if she'd ever talked to someone so old. Her grandparents had died when she was still very young.

Grandmother waved one hand at the plate of cookies impatiently, cradling the cup against her bosom. Alyson handed her another shortbread square.

"I could eat these all day long. Who are you again? Not another nurse, are you?"

"No, ma'am, I'm with Marcus. I mean, no, not *with* Marcus, but he invited me."

"Where's Marcus? Is he here? Oh, Milton and I spoiled that boy. Two peas in a pod they were. It tore little Marcus up when my Milty died. Once the diabetes got hold of him, it was all but over. Infections, cut off his toes, cut off his foot. Stayed joyful for everybody by the grace of God. I alone knew how pained he was." Her eyes grew bright with pooling tears. "Thought it would just about kill little Marcus watching his gramps die piece by piece like that."

Alyson wondered if that was the reason behind all the sad photos of Marcus when he was a teenager. And then the sudden weight loss and body-building. Yes, watching his beloved gramps die had affected him, deeply.

"But, Edinburgh. I was telling you about Edinburgh because these cookies and this tea remind me of a night we had there that was magical. Just *magical*." She took a long sip of her tea then held it out for Alyson to take. She did and set it on the table for her.

"So we'd honeymooned in Dublin. Still a small town back then, and we'd been able to rent a room over a bar for nearly a whole week because he'd played with the man's brother in New York. Matter of fact, the reason it was our honeymoon was that I told Milty he wasn't about to leave me at home while he went gallivanting off having adventures without me. So, after six weeks of courtin', we up and married, and he took me with him. And what adventures we had!"

"Only six weeks?" Alyson hadn't meant to interrupt and regretted it as Grandmother looked at her as if seeing her for the first time. Alyson handed her the tea cup, hoping that would center the woman on an activity.

"What do you mean 'only six weeks'? That's a lifetime when you're in love."

"How did you know he was *the one*?"

"Little girl, when you know, you just know. You think, 'that's *my* man, and nothing less will do' and you go for it." She took a long drink of her tea, then handed it back. "Where was I?"

"Honeymoon in Dublin? Edinburgh?"

"Oh, yes, yes. Milty was always restless, a wanderer. We hopped the ferry and went to London Town. He performed a few gigs, giving us enough money to extend our trip *another* few weeks. Such a hoot! He always trusted God would provide, and He always, *always* did, just when we needed it. Everything was an adventure with Milty.

"So we went up to Edinburgh on the train. It was dark and cold, and hardly anyone was out on that Royal Mile. We saw a sign that said there were rooms to let over this pub, so we walked into a dark, dank room that seemed to have no one there at all except for the movement in the shadows. The bartender barked out 'We don't want any.' Milty asked about the room for let. 'No rooms here.' Bark bark bark. But Milty never took that from people. He said, 'Yes, sir, the place looks full to the brim. Looks like you've had to turn people away all night.' Oh, the glare from that red-nosed bulldog of a barman. I thought we were in trouble! Then Milty said, 'Tell you what. When I make you some money, you give me and my wife a room for the night. It's just too late to go anywhere else.' The bartender, big barrel chest, comes around the bar. Looked at first like he was going to throw us out, but I could see dollar signs in his eyes. 'And how do you propose that?' he said. And that's when Milty took out his violin and began to play.

"Not even fifteen seconds of Bluegrass and the bar man told his little son to spread word far and wide that a black Yankee was going to bring down the house tonight." She laughed, hand on heart. "Here I was, thinking we were about to be food for the lions, but the people came—*with their instruments*—and they had a jamboree all night long. That was my Milty. He could bring strangers together in a heartbeat." She shook her head with pride.

Alyson saw movement in the doorway and looked up to see Marcus, Marianne and Dottie. The grandmother followed her gaze over her shoulder and turned to see them standing there.

"Dorothy, you need to get this little girl's recipe. This tastes just like the shortbread and tea I had in Edinburgh all those years ago. I must've eaten nothing but shortbread, and oh! That bread pudding chock full of currants." She raised her hand to the ceiling like she was praising the Almighty. "Oh Mercy! We were such children, eating dessert for every meal, just because we could." Her almost constant laughter had everyone smiling.

"Yes, *Maman*, I will." Dottie gave her mother a sideways hug on her shoulders and mouthed a teary "Thank you" to Alyson.

Marcus came and sat backward on a chair. "What happened next, *Mere-mere*?"

"Why, we women danced, Marcus! We danced and danced like the Holy Ghost had our feet. We were invited to parties, and there was music and dancing non-stop."

Alyson grabbed her phone and brought up a traditional circle dance. "Was it something like this?"

Grandmother clapped her hands together like a prayer, her smile so bright. Alyson grabbed

Marianne and danced with her, Marianne stiff, but trying.

"Hey, where'd everyone go?" Gail arrived with Darius and Andre, both boys looking worried. But Alyson saw recognition flash on Darius's face, and he came zooming into the kitchen and danced with her like she and her mom had taught him. Gail joined the circle.

"This a weird Cotton-Eyed Joe?" Gail asked.

Alyson laughed. "It's the grandpa of all Cotton-Eyed Joes. Time to turn!" She grabbed Darius's hands, and they turned in a circle, leaning out, going faster and faster. This was his favorite part. "Now face your partner." Alyson and Darius put hands on hips and performed the fancy footwork most people left out.

"Oh, it's one of those Irish tap dance things." Gail stood back.

"Time for the circle." Alyson waved them to follow, and they did. She made a loop around the kitchen with Darius, side-by-side. Grandmother stood, and Marcus and Dottie helped her to the middle, and they shuffled along too. Alyson called for them to open the circle, so all of them were part of it, holding hands, and she slowed the dance to something Grandmother could take part in.

Gail turned it into a line dance with deep shoulder moves and a snaking body.

"Now we're talking." Marianne followed Gail. Darius followed too.

Marcus added drumbeats on the table, turning the old music new.

The dance had become a new creation, and Alyson followed the new, smoother, less feverish dance. *When in Rome . . .*

Grandmother's smile and laughter couldn't get any bigger. Tears of joy rolled down Dottie's cheeks.

They felt like one. One moving body, one with the music, one in Love. And when the song ended, Dottie and her mom hugged and hugged, like Grandmother had been away on a long trip. Her grandchildren surrounded her, each hugging her in turn.

"Marcus, your girl is an angel of delight. Grandpa would be so proud you'd found a nice girl to share your music with."

Marcus looked down, guilty. He seemed about to correct his grandmother, so Alyson stepped forward, stopping him with a hand on his arm.

"See, Marcus, I'm an angel of delight, and don't you forget it." His sisters laughed. Then more seriously, Alyson turned to Grandmother and said, "Thank you for sharing your story with me."

"Oh, darling girl, if you only knew how much I had to say. It just gets stuck sometimes." Her gaze turned inward.

Alyson thought it best to keep the distractions going. "How would you like to watch the children make s'mores by the fire?"

Grandmother laughed and shuffled that way, grasping onto Gail's arm for support. "As long as I don't have to clean it up!"

Dottie crossed to Alyson and gathered her into a bear hug. "Thank you thank you thank you, Jesus, for bringing our girl Alyson to wake up *Maman*. There are so few good days for her, and this is the best." Dottie kissed her cheek, wetting Alyson's face with her tears. "Thank you for being kind to my mama, sweet girl. Listening to her, entertaining her. You've a heart of gold."

The sound of Grandmother's laughter floated to them, and Dottie followed it, gracing Alyson with one more beaming smile before she left.

"Aren't you coming?" Marcus stopped in the doorway.

"Not without the tea and cookies. Let's keep this party going for your grandma. Help me find a tray?"

Chapter Thirteen

That night they listened to Grandmother tell her stories by the fire until she tired. As long as she was talking about her life when she was in her twenties and thirties, everything was all right. But toward the end of the night, she wondered how late it was and when Milty would get home.

"Okay, *Maman*. Maybe it's time for bed now." Dottie helped her mother stand and walked with her arm in arm toward the hall to the bedrooms. The last Alyson heard was Grandmother saying, "But I don't want to miss Milty. I want to hear all about his latest trip."

"Me too, *Maman*. I promise I'll wake you if I see him."

It was enough to break your heart. Alyson felt the sting of tears beginning. That's what she wanted—a love so deep and true it survived death and dementia. She should never have settled for Will. She should have waited for real love, not just infatuation. But she hadn't known the difference back then.

"You okay?" Marcus touched her arm to get her attention. "You've been so quiet since we all moved to the great room."

"I'm fine. Just thinking"–*about the past*–"about the future. I don't think Mom is coming home. She's asking me to manage the sale for her."

"Grandma's not coming home?" Darius came up beside her. Last she'd seen, a small group of boys had been playing with *Star Wars* action figures behind the other loveseat. She wouldn't have said anything if she'd known he could hear.

"I don't know. But we'll get another chance to talk with her later tonight or tomorrow. She was at a restaurant, so it was hard to hear." She wasn't sure why she lied, but it sounded better than "Grandma was having too much fun to talk to a downer like me."

"A restaurant? On Christmas?" Darius screwed up his face. "Is that a *thing*?"

She and Marcus both laughed. "Spoken like a true New Yorker." She hugged her boy. "Yes, I think that's a *thing* in San Diego. For those who can afford it, anyway."

"I want to come *here* next Christmas. And Moses said they have a big party in July too. Can we come for that?"

"Darius. We'll see what the future brings, okay?"

He was immediately glum, then brightened again. "Did Dad call yet? When's he going to call?"

Her lungs burned. How best to lie to her child? "I don't know when he'll call, sweetheart. You know there's a time difference, and it's already pretty late there. Maybe tomorrow." She wished Will hadn't called on Darius's birthday. He was just jerking them around.

He scowled at her like she was the one keeping his dad from calling him. "Are we at least having lasagna? When's it going to be ready?"

That warmed her heart. Her boy was as much a stickler for tradition as she was. "No, baby, we had the big meal already. It's just snacks while we play games."

"Lasagna?" Marcus asked. "Where'd that come from?"

"We always have lasagna Christmas night. I'm half Italian. It's a tradition. Lasagna, panettone, Swiss chocolates, and marzipan."

"And tea and shortbread," Gail added.

"The other half is Irish. Well, Scots-Irish to be exact. They hopped the Irish Sea every other generation. I'm a San Antonio native, though."

"Huh." Gail stepped in behind Darius and sat on the ottoman. "Huh" seemed to be Gail's main expression of interest. "So what you're saying is, you're a mafia leprechaun."

As if she hadn't heard that one before. She had a shtick ready.

Alyson paraphrased famous mafia movie lines in a stereotypical Irish accent. "I'll make you an offer you can't refuse. You talkin' to me? You think I'm funny? I'm a clown to you?"

She had the guys in the room roaring and the women laughing nervously. Then she switched and quoted the Lucky Charms commercial in the voice of The Godfather. Uncle Mason was about to have a hernia, he was laughing so hard. *Two points for team Stefanelli.*

"Lasagna tomorrow night, then," Marcus said still smiling. "We'll go pick up all the ingredients, and then celebrate the sale of your car with a big fat lasagna."

"Does anyone here even like lasagna?"

"All in favor of lasagna, say aye," Marcus announced. Everyone in the room, adults and kids alike, called out, "aye." Marcus said, "All opposed say nay." Moses bleated like a jackass, making all the adults laugh. It seemed she wasn't the only one trying to rack up laughter points. It was the sport of the household.

She smiled and pushed Marcus. "You're just trying to get me to stay another night, so I'll go to church with you on Sunday." He always reacted to her pushing like it tickled, which made her want to do it more.

"Is it working?" He grabbed her hands so she couldn't keep pushing him.

"Yeah."

"Good. That's half the reason I wanted you to come for Christmas."

"Ugh. Y'all are sickening." Gail got up from the ottoman and left.

Marcus dropped her hands and muttered an apology.

She wasn't sure why Gail's reaction bothered him so much. Did he think he was taking liberties? They were just playing. After an awkward moment, she said, "I better go find Andre. He's probably getting sleepy."

He sprang up from the ultra-soft leather couch and offered his hand to help her up. "I think they're coloring in the kitchen."

"Thanks." She would miss this gentlemanly attention when they returned to normal life. Would they ever see each other again after Sunday? Maybe that's why he was already pulling back. She put the thought out of her mind, as it was too depressing for now. She didn't want the future, only the present.

෨ඐ

"You going to bed already?" Marcus was at the open bedroom door. "Oh sorry."

She waved him in, but continued to sing a lullaby to her baby, who was getting so big. Andre took a deep breath and let it out without opening his eyes. He was almost asleep.

Marcus stood behind her and began singing too, very softly, his hand on her shoulder. It was one of those moments that pained her heart—this should have happened with their father, and it never had. She vowed right then, that if she ever remarried, it would be to a nurturer like Marcus, not a power-hungry child like her ex. But she was prepared for loneliness—it was the best way, the narrow path.

Her voice faltered, but Marcus finished the song for his audience of one. Andre was asleep.

"That was beautiful," she said. "You should sing *me* to sleep."

"Give me where and when. I'll be there."

Another one of those awkward moments that might be flirting, or might just be Marcus being Marcus. Better to ignore it. She led him out of the room, keeping the door open so she could hear if Andre called out.

She heard people near the front door. Heard Dottie saying goodbye to folks. "Where's everyone going?"

"Not everyone sleeps here, you know. Just the out-of-towners and the grandkids mom watches over Christmas break. We'll see everybody again on Sunday."

Everyone else was in the kitchen, and as they approached, Alyson heard something that made her middle sink. Marcus singing for Della department store.

Marcus heard it too and sped into the kitchen.

Darius, Gail and Moses were watching a video on Gail's phone.

Gail looked up when Marcus came in. "What are you wearing in this?" Gail laughed and showed the phone to the others hanging out near the table. They too laughed. "You're the Jolly Green Giant!"

"Turn that off!" Marcus growled.

Darius looked terrified. Then his face fell like it was the end of his world. Alyson went to comfort him, and he buried his face in her side.

Gail held the phone out of Marcus's reach. He'd have to climb over the table to get it. He looked tempted.

"What's all the ruckus in here?" Dottie came in from the foyer, her eyes drawn to the video that played.

Marcus looked from his mom to where his dad and Uncle Mason were standing over by the coffee maker. All the fight went out of Marcus. The hang of his head showed he knew it was too late to stop the inevitable.

"I didn't want y'all to see that."

"Why not? It's beautiful singing, Marcus." Dottie put her hand out for the phone, and Gail handed it to her.

"Yeah, there's nothing better than a big black elf singing, 'Here Comes Santa Claus,' and clapping his hands like he's down on the farm."

"Gail," Dottie warned.

"See, Mama? That's *exactly* why I didn't want y'all to see it."

"You're so ashamed of it, why'd you do it?" Gail countered.

"How do you think paid for all the gifts I brought?"

"But, son, you said you were doing all right." His dad stepped forward.

"You didn't need a second job to buy gifts for us, baby." Dottie walked through the group to her husband and put a hand on his arm as if to stop him from approaching his son. "We just want you to come visit more often."

"Are you having trouble paying your bills?" His dad looked over his glasses at Marcus, and after setting his coffee cup on the counter, stepped closer. Dottie tugged his arm. He pulled away.

"No, Dad. I'm fine."

"I saw that article in the paper about plans to cut music programs in schools. You should move back home, son. Where you have a network."

"No! No." Marcus stood palms out, halting everyone. "The whole reason I don't ever tell y'all anything is because you always second-guess me. Like I can't make it on my own, much less be a success. I'm *doing* this. I'm just doing it at my pace."

"Son, there are good-paying jobs here in the church." Marcus's dad stepped away from Dottie who was now pulling on his arm in a blatant attempt to stop him. "We need a new musical director for the praise team, and ... and, son, there's something else I've been meaning—"

"Dad. Please. Music is my calling. But preaching to the choir isn't. My gifts belong out there. I will do this on my own."

Alyson raised a brow—he had mocked her in the mall parking garage with that same phrase: "I'll do this on my own." She knew better than to get involved in a family squabble, but she'd have a mouthful for the hypocrite after she saw Darius to bed.

She looked around for Darius—he was gone. If he'd run out of the kitchen, she would have noticed. No, he's not under the table. She went farther in the kitchen and looked in the corners and under the small desk. Nothing. "Darius? Where are you, sweetie?"

Marcus stood beside her. He opened a pocket door to a laundry room. She saw Darius's sneakers poking out from under a folding table next to the dryer.

"Darius, it's okay, sweetie. No one's mad at you." She sat on the floor and moved aside the curtain ruffle that hid Darius's face.

"He hates me now, just like Daddy. Everyone hates me." Darius let loose a fresh bout of tears and sobs.

"That's not true. Come here." She opened her arms, and he launched himself into them, almost knocking her over. As big as he was for an eight-year-old, he collapsed himself into her lap, and she rocked him as he cried into her shoulder. "You *are* loved. I love you so much."

"You *have* to love me. No one else does." His muffled words spurred a fresh bout of sobs.

Marcus squatted and rubbed Darius's shoulder. "Darius, I could *never* hate you. You're my 'Number One,' my best." He lifted Darius's chin slightly. "Of course I love you. I just can't say it out loud because I'm your teacher—I can't play favorites."

They stayed like that a while, Darius's crying becoming softer and softer as he grew to believe them.

Darius unfolded himself and sat back against the washing machine. "Why don't you want them to know you worked at the mall?" His voice was small and mumbly and hard to hear. "Why is it a bad place? Mom works there."

"It's not a bad place. I just want to keep it private."

"But why? You did a good thing. You've got to tell your mom about the good stuff. So she's proud of you."

Marcus hung his head. "You're right, Dare. You're absolutely right. You shouldn't hide anything from your parents."

"So why did you?"

Marcus sighed and looked at Alyson. She shrugged.

"It's complicated, little man."

Darius screwed up his face like the word stank. "That's what Dad always says. I bet that's why he didn't call. *It's complicated.*"

Alyson had heard that phrase too many times to count. The phrase used when her ex was selfish and tried to excuse his behavior. And now Marcus. She was better off staying single forever. At least she'd never have to hear that stupid phrase again, and neither would her sons.

"Mama Dottie." Moses stood behind Dottie just outside the laundry room, pulling on her sleeve. "We need the Fortress of Solitude."

"Okay but turn on the lights and wear your jackets. I'll make you boys some hot chocolate to take to the fortress. Now, where's that old thermos?" Dottie turned toward a high cupboard.

Moses waved for Darius, and they ran through the house together, Moses yelling, "To the Fortress of Solitude!" and the other boys hollering along.

Marcus stood and helped Alyson up.

Instead of leaving, she closed the pocket door, sealing them inside the small space together. Surprise lit up Marcus's face. She let her tight lips and narrowed eyes do the talking.

"I'm sorry, Alyson. I didn't think he'd react that way."

"I'm not mad at you for that. No one has helped him more than you have. I'm mad because you made fun of me for wanting to do things on my own, but then you say the exact same thing? So you think I can't do this on my own because I'm a woman, but you can because you're a man?"

"What? When did I say that?"

"Just a few minutes ago, you said you would do it all on your own, and you don't want help from anybody. So what was all this talk about letting people help me? You think I'm weak? I'm not listening to you anymore, Mr. Double Standard."

"No, you're missing my point."

"And what is your point? You care more about your image than anything else. That's why you didn't want anyone to see those videos. You're ashamed of something that *meant a lot* to me." She covered her heart with both hands. "You saved the day and made so many people happy, but all you care about is your precious image. It's not *complicated* at all." She squared off with burning eyes and clenched teeth. So why did she feel so sad? She swallowed, unable to hold the anger.

Like sand pouring through her, itchy and chaffing, came the realization of where the anger belonged. Will. Old resentments rose like acid in her throat. She swallowed them back. She couldn't speak.

Marcus rubbed up and down her arms. "Alyson, I don't think you're talking to me right now." He held her shoulders until she met his gaze. "I'm not your ex."

She hung her head. So pathetic and transparent that Marcus could call her out. All the hate and blame and tension of the past six months wanted her to break down and she wouldn't let it happen, not here, not now. She hid her face from Marcus and tried to get a hold of herself.

"Listen. Here's the whole truth." Marcus spoke softly as he leaned against the washing machine and lifted her chin gently to get her to meet his eye, just as he had done to Darius. "I liked being an elf, and I liked working with you. I like trying to figure you out. But I only had that job because getting my band's van fixed took all of my Christmas money. And I wasn't about to touch the money I've been saving to move to L.A. I don't *dare* ever ask my parents for money because I know they are always helping at least three or four families from the church. If they help me, they can't help them."

She sniffed and nodded. Of course. Of course he would have perfectly good reasons for everything he did. Of course his reasoning would show him to be magnanimous and forthright and all other good things she was finding annoying right now.

He continued. "My independence is about creating who I want to be, committing to my dreams. Your independence is building up walls to keep everyone out, including me, and I will not let you do that." He tried to hold her hand, but she pulled it away.

"First of all"—she pressed her finger into his chest—"I'm sick of you being right all the time. Can't you ever mess up? I mean, really, no one is this perfect. Second, I admit I've built up walls, but they are there to keep *me together*, not to keep you out. And third, I finally get it. The *real* reason you invited us here was that you think you can *fix* me. Well, you just back off, boy-o, because I'm no one's *pet project*." She slid open the pocket door expecting an empty kitchen, but instead, walked into the room with almost all of Marcus's family watching, like her life was a *telenovela*. They'd heard everything.

She marched into the bedroom where Andre lay sleeping. She paced, grinding her teeth. *The nerve of him.*

She'd paced back and forth a few times, wishing she'd brought her running gear so she could let off steam, when she noticed the present on the dresser. It was the same wrapping paper as all the gifts Marcus had brought with him. When had he put that in here? He must have done it when she was putting Andre to sleep.

She picked it up—it was heavy and square, solid. Haphazardly wrapped, it included a note lodged in the bow:

"I left this in the car by accident. Sorry you didn't have a gift to open this morning. But now it has even more meaning. When you light it, I hope you remember the gift you gave my mom tonight when you shared your tea and cookies with my grandmother. –Marcus"

She opened it. A large, scented candle. Bergamot. She took a deep whiff of the scent. It smelled like the spice in her afternoon tea . . . and was that tantalizing mystery ingredient in Marcus's cologne that had had her sniffing him like an animal in the car.

So which came first: his cologne, or the knowledge that she liked the scent? Either way, the sentiment in the note melted her anger completely. It was impossible to stay angry at this man.

Without her anger, she was defenseless.

She lit the candle with matches he had also provided, filling the room with his scent.

Defenseless.

Chapter Fourteen

Alyson spied Gail in her PJs crossing to the kitchen with a steaming cup of coffee in hand. She tied her silky robe and slipped into the hall, tiptoeing after Gail. She found her adding more sugar to her cup.

"Good morning."

Gail jumped, the second spoonful of sugar feathering out over the countertop. "Girl, make a noise or something! You scared me half to death."

"Sorry. Are we the only ones up?"

"Yeah. Surprise, surprise. Mama's usually up before dawn, but all the excitement last night with *Mere-mere* had Mama chatting half the night, reliving the whole thing." She wiped the sugar from the counter into her hand and threw it in the sink. "That was cool, by the way. Dancing in the kitchen like that. Mama loved it. Made everyone feel young again, not just *Mere-mere*."

Alyson didn't know what to say. Everyone made it into such a big deal, but it was a natural thing for her. What else would she have done?

"And then I went and made a fool of myself." Alyson sat on a stool at the counter.

"Really?" Gail looked wide-eyed. "I hadn't noticed."

Alyson laughed.

"If you ask me"—Gail gesticulated with her spoon—"the only one of us who behaved with total honesty and purity of heart was Darius. I was a jerk. Marcus was a jerk."

"I was a jerk."

"No, girl. You're just funny." She mimicked Alyson's higher voice, quoting her from the previous night. "'I'm sick of you being *right* all the time.' Now you know how I felt growing up with Little Mr. Perfect. Sure is dependable though. Huggable, lovable, teddy bear Marcus. Hard to measure up against all that when you're snarky, cantankerous, thorny old Gail." She took a sip of her coffee and grimaced at it.

"The coffee is horrible. I made it. I guess I've gotten too used to my coffee pods. Why Mama doesn't get a modern coffeepot, I'll never know. Percolator. That thing's ancient."

Gail took another sip of her coffee, then poured it down the sink. "How about this: you make the coffee, and I'll get pancakes and sausage started. That'll give Mama a break this morning, let her sleep in."

"Wonderful idea!" She would love to make it all better again. Guests shouldn't cause problems like this—she didn't want Dottie to think she was ungrateful.

They got right to it, still in their pajamas and nightgown, drinking coffee and flipping flapjacks as others woke up and stumbled toward the yummy aromas.

Marcus approached with a small army of boys, including Darius and Moses, who now seemed inseparable. There were fewer people than the day before, just family now.

"Good morning, ladies." Marcus took plates from the dishwasher and stacked them near the food on the counter. "Jayden, pancakes are not tacos, use a plate. You get syrup on the floor, you're mopping."

Alyson glanced at the teen boy who had put sausage and syrup in the folded pancake, dripping syrup on the counter while the younger boys laughed.

Marcus turned back toward them, dressed in an undershirt and basketball shorts, his feet bare and his beard scruffy. She liked seeing him like this—relaxed and at home.

"Better flip them. They're ready." Gail stood next to her at a second electric griddle cooking the sausage patties. Her teasing tone meant she'd caught Alyson checking out Marcus.

"Right. I'm on it." She flipped the four pancakes, the heat of embarrassment crawling up her neck. They were supposed to be just friends, and the fight yesterday proved it. There was nothing between them. At all. Even if she had fallen asleep surrounded by his scent. She closed her eyes, taking a time-out. *I'm such a mess. I know what's right, so why is this so hard?*

And yet, she couldn't help but feel him everywhere he went in the kitchen—as he got his coffee, added cream from the fridge, stepped back for a spoon—it was like they were connected by a million tiny little strings, and she sensed them move and stretch as he went away or came closer. Maddening . . . But she liked it. Liked being that in tune with someone. She wished it didn't have to end.

She poured more batter onto the griddle, then turned to him. He seemed to have been waiting for her to do so.

"Thank you for the candle. I love it."

His eyes smiled over his coffee cup. "I'm glad." His gaze flowed from her head to her toes, drinking her in. "You attend the opera in your sleep? You sure you want to cook in that?"

She smiled, bowing her head. The silk and lace nighty and robe seemed fancy, but they were old and comfortable. "It's all right. How did you know I like bergamot?"

"You're a creature of habit."

"What do you mean?"

He stepped closer. "As long as I've known you, you've had an afternoon break with the same Earl Grey tea. Must admit I was jealous of the time you spent with the Earl. You never wanted company on your breaks."

"I'm sorry, Marcus. I must have seemed like an ice queen the way I treated all of you."

"You did what you had to, I guess." He held out his hand for the spatula.

She gave it to him, stepping away to allow him to take over.

"I'm glad you don't feel you have to ice us out anymore, though. I like the new you."

"I haven't changed."

He peered at her from the corner of his eye, a sly smile playing on his lips. "You've changed enough to let people see the *real* you." He waved the spatula at her. "Don't argue. I'll win this one."

Hands up in surrender, she said, "I give up, don't flip me!"

He glanced from the spatula to her, an evil grin alighting on his face, just as she'd hoped. He chased her around the kitchen with the spatula, both laughing, the boys at the table shouting, "Run" and "Get her." Gail yelled, "Come back with that spatula, you thief!" The boys piled on Marcus to see who could get the spatula. Alyson waved and ran off toward the bedroom to shower and dress.

She wanted to look her best. Big day today. She'd only end up with a simple check or an electronic deposit, but in her mind, it was *bushels* of cash from the sale of her car. Now it was time, she couldn't wait.

Getting rid of her ex-husband's gift would be one more step toward true freedom.

৵৹৵

"You're just in time. Come. Sit and eat." Dottie waved her over. Now only Dottie, Gail, Marcus, his dad and Marianne, sat at the table together, enjoying the last of the breakfast. "Marcus just told us your plan for the day."

She sat at the head of the table where Dottie had indicated. "I might be too nervous to eat. I think I should go wipe out the interior of the car again."

"There will be time for that later." Marcus grabbed the casserole dish that kept the food warm and loaded up Alyson's plate with more than she could eat.

She smiled her thanks to him.

As he sat back down, he said, "Marianne will watch the boys for us while we take care of the sale."

"Thank you so much!" Alyson embraced Marianne with a look of gratitude. "It will be a huge help not having to keep up with a squirmy Andre while we find a used car." *Why did Marianne chuckle and shake her head?*

Alyson saw Marcus's mom and dad exchange a look. Alyson glanced at Marcus and could tell that he had seen it too. He shrugged. She shrugged back.

Marianne stifled a laugh, even putting her hand in front of her mouth.

"What?" Marcus said.

"Nothing. You two are something else is all. Something else."

His parents exchanged another look, smiling.

Marcus's raised eyebrows and wide eyes told her, *I don't know what's up. Whatever.* She believed him.

Marianne and Gail now laughed out loud.

"What!" Marcus's tone had a hint of irritation, but it didn't stop him from chuckling along with his sisters' giggles.

His dad cleared his throat. "Alyson. Sorry, we've had little chance to talk." He reached across the table to shake her hand. "You can call me Charles."

"Thank you, Charles, it's a pleasure to meet you." The sudden seriousness of Marcus, Gail and Marianne revealed it was a big deal that he'd introduced himself this way.

"Tell me a little about yourself."

Uh-oh. This now seemed like an interview. "Oh. Well, you've seen Darius and Andre running around here. My boys are my life." She breathed out heavily and cast her gaze down, trying to figure out what else to say. She never talked about herself.

"My mom is Irish, born north of Dublin. She came to the states in the 70s when the Troubles made Ireland too dangerous. She was a receptionist, recently retired. My dad was from New Jersey but left when he joined the Army at seventeen. I have no surviving grandparents. My twin, Amy, lives in California and just had a baby girl. Amy teaches literature at a small college." She glanced at Charles, who had a knowing smile. Somehow, she must be failing. "I guess that's it. There's not much to tell."

"So, now we know you're a family-oriented person. That's great. Now, what about *you*? Who are *you*?" Charles's voice was gentle and held a hint of humor, but it still registered as probing.

How should she define herself if not by her role in life? She was a mom and daughter, sister and . . . well, not even a very good friend. Housewares manager certainly didn't define her. There was nothing else to say. She had to be the least interesting person alive.

"Let the poor girl eat." Dottie patted her shoulder.

Marcus got up from the bench, coffee mug in hand. "She's an efficient manager, a fierce opponent in b-ball, amazing dancer, kind helper, fun mom, and a tell-it-like-it-is confidant." Then to her, "You want coffee?"

She could've kissed him.

He nodded and brought down another mug from the cupboard.

She noted another look exchanged between Dottie and Charles. Dottie's smile only widened when she met Alyson's gaze. What was going on here? Something was definitely going on. Alyson and Marcus seemed to be the only ones not in on the joke.

She took a bite of the pancakes though she was too nervous to be hungry. The vanilla, cinnamon and pecans Gail had added to the batter were a nice touch. She took another bite. Marcus delivered her coffee then bumped against Gail with his hip, signaling she needed to move down the bench and make room for him next to Alyson. He didn't look her way but sat and sipped his coffee.

"Where do you go to church?" Charles asked.

All eyes were on him. Then all eyes were on her.

"I don't."

Dottie gasped and looked at Marcus, not her, with disbelief. Gail and Marianne were both wide-eyed, with "uh-oh!" clear on their faces. Maybe she wasn't as welcome as she'd thought. Yet Charles's expression never changed from thoughtful curiosity.

Marcus hung his head and sighed. "Dad, come on. This isn't necessary."

"It's okay. I don't mind." She kept her voice light and perky. She didn't want Marcus to feel any worse, especially after he'd been so kind, and she'd been so rotten to him last night. "I haven't attended regularly since my teens. I attended mass every Wednesday, Friday and Sunday from kinder to ninth grade, so I figured I had enough saved up for a while."

Gail snorted laughter.

"Catholic," Marianne announced with a smile, as if an Irish-Italian being Catholic was some kind of surprise.

Charles ignored the others. He looked intrigued, as if she were a riddle. "Why did you stop?"

"My father died." She shrugged. "My mom fell apart."

Dottie was the first to respond with sympathy, and the others followed suit.

"It's okay. I'm sorry, I didn't mean to sound so dramatic. It's just . . . when Daddy died we no longer had money for private school. Dad had been a deacon, so Mom couldn't attend mass without breaking down. Amy too. She and Mom were both hit pretty hard. We stopped going. Stopped everything." She put down her fork.

"The longer we were away, the easier it was not to go. Once Mom was okay again, my sister and I focused on getting scholarships for college. Church was just part of the 'before,' and we were living in the 'after.'"

Dottie rubbed her arm. "It must have been hard having to be the strong one for your family."

Alyson opened her mouth to assure her it hadn't been hard—but it had. The words of assurance died on her tongue as she found herself back in her mother's dark bedroom, setting a tray of food and tea on the foot of the bed and shaking her mother gently as if to wake her, though Alyson could clearly see her red-rimmed eyes staring at the wall. "Mom, your work called again. I told them you had the flu. I didn't know what else to say."

"I never should've gone back to work." Her mom barely breathed the words. "I wasn't ready."

"Mom, it's been almost six months—"

"Didn't you love your father?" Her mom yelled, gripping Alyson's wrist with ice-cold fingers. She sat up, kicking the dishes and the tray to the floor. "Why aren't you suffering?" She let go and fell back to her pillow, face half-hidden, sobbing. "Why aren't you suffering?"

Alyson, aware that Marcus's family looked on patiently, spoke her epiphany before she'd fully realized it: "Having to be the one in charge broke my relationship with my mother." Hearing the words was strange, but they felt true. "We never could get it back, the mother-daughter thing. We've been . . . competitors . . . ever since."

Dottie patted her hand, and Alyson briefly covered it with her own. "I've gotten more mothering this weekend than I have in over a decade."

Dottie pulled her in for a gentle hug. "And you are welcome here anytime." Then her expression sobered. "You know, as long as both you and your mama are alive, whatever's torn between you can be mended. It's not too late."

Alyson sighed. "I don't know, Dottie. There's always been a distance between us. We never speak of the dark times."

"Maybe she feels guilty for not being strong enough," Marianne offered.

"And guilt almost always turns to resentment. I know *that* firsthand," Gail added.

"It was weird," Alyson continued. "She was angry that I didn't break down when Daddy died. But the break between us happened when I told her why."

Charles leaned in, genuinely interested. Alyson had almost forgotten he was there he had been so still. Marcus too.

"I considered myself the lucky one. I felt my dad's love as strongly after he died as I did before. It just seemed we couldn't communicate the same way. I knew what to do because he'd taught me. I missed him, but I wasn't focused on his absence like my mom and sister were. They couldn't help themselves. It was all they felt. His absence."

"Huh. Yeah." Charles looked off to the side but seemed to be looking inward. "They felt only his absence," he muttered, scratching his chin. "But you followed his example. Yes." He appeared to be staring into mid-air, but laser focused.

"There he goes," Gail said. "Bye, Dad."

"Go on to your computer, Charlie." Dottie took his plate and added it on top of hers. "You've got your composing face on. Book or sermon?"

"Book." He stood and kissed his wife's cheek, then came and stood behind Alyson and squeezed her shoulders. "Welcome, Alyson. Welcome. Forgive my rudeness." Two steps away, he turned to say with a smile, "And thank you!"

She returned the smile, then he left. "What did I say?"

"Who knows, honey." Dottie got up with the plates, but Marianne and Gail took over for her. Dottie sat back down.

"He's writing a book about the apostles after the resurrection, and how confused they all were. He was stuck, and something you said got him unstuck." Dottie reached out and squeezed her hand. "Looks like you were meant to be here. Again. You're having quite an effect on this family."

Chapter Fifteen

"Why don't y'all roam around while I finalize the paperwork with the buyers." Uncle Mason dismissed them by tossing keys without looking up. Marcus caught them and smiled at his uncle—just like old times.

Marcus bounced the keys in his right hand and led her out of the office with his left hand at her back. She didn't seem to mind. The more delicate he treated her, the more delicate she became. It amazed him how comfortable they were around each other now, as if their fight last night had opened something.

"What he really meant was he wants me to show you the Toyota he wants off his lot." He jingled the keys. "But if something else catches your eye, we can test drive that one too."

"We're going to test drive now?"

"Sure. I used to work here. My first job. Washing cars all summer long." He guided her to the back of the lot where the non-luxury cars were. "What was your first job?"

"You won't believe me."

"What? You did something crazy?"

"No. My first job was with Mr. Giles at Della. Every summer. After the divorce, I ran straight back to where I'd been. I didn't even try for anything else. I guess I was scared. Certainly desperate."

"You must've been happy there."

"I was. Everyone treated me like a kid sister. Mr. Giles helped me decide on business administration when I couldn't choose a major. Said it was a good foundation for anything."

Marcus opened the driver's door for her and handed her the keys.

"This is so weird. I'm almost thirty and I've never bought a car before. I feel like a child."

He leaned over the door. "Uncle Mason will make this a piece of cake. Don't fret."

"*Fret*. I haven't fretted a day in my life. My mother would say 'quit your whining.' I like 'don't fret' better."

He returned her smile and closed her door, then crossed to the passenger side. It took some maneuvering, but he got comfortable in the small seat. He watched her nervously adjusting her mirrors. "Whenever you're ready, make a right out of here and I'll tell you where to drive so we make a loop."

They drove for about ten minutes, adjusting to the new brakes her only problem. He'd been guiding them toward a green space where he hoped they'd have time to talk, just the two of them. Time was short now that the car deals were being made— she could leave at any time. He had to know what was happening between them before she left or it would be too late. "Next right. Let's pull over here."

She obeyed and gasped as the buildings gave way to a beautiful wooded area. He looked on in surprise too. The simple green space he'd known years ago was now a full-fledged park with walking trails, benches, a small playground—and way too many people for them to have the conversation he wanted to have.

She hopped out as soon as she'd put the car in park, gleefully bouncing on the balls of her feet as she pointed to the trees and small pond. She said something and smiled, but he couldn't hear. He caught up to her, enjoying the crisp fresh air and her bright smile.

"Weeping willows! I love weeping willows. What a great little park. I wish the boys were here. Let's go take a look." She grabbed his hand and pulled him along, but when she made to let go, he changed the grip, intertwining their fingers.

She didn't resist but walked beside him more reserved than before. He'd give anything to know what she was thinking when she went quiet. He might've taken it too far, but she'd matched his grip. Maybe there was something there?

When they reached the trees, he let her go, and she danced in the midst of the low-hanging branches.

"It was always so sad to see the willows losing their leaves up north. The harbinger of winter and long, lonely nights. But it's like perpetual summer here." She brushed the low-hanging leaves with her hand, as if touching the hair of a dear one.

The loving glow on her face over such a simple thing made his heart ache. "You're a nature-lover."

"Very much so. Or at least, I used to be." She turned her head toward the pond. "Did I hear ducks? Shouldn't they have flown south or something? Come on."

"We are south." He chuckled and followed her to the pond, now so surrounded by trees and field you wouldn't know the city was just beyond. Most of the people were by the playground—he had privacy under this green canopy—so he tried to muster the courage to speak. And couldn't.

Instead, he bumped her hand twice with his own as they walked, but she didn't take it. He wouldn't force it. Only friends, after all.

She turned to him, stopping him with a hand on his arm. "I'm sorry. I meant to do this earlier . . . apologize for last night." She held his gaze while trying to tame her hair blown in the breeze. "You aren't trying to *fix* me, you're just being kind."

His stomach bottomed out—*even kindness can be cruel.* His father was right. This thing he'd started by inviting her here would hurt them both. Yes, he'd been leading her on. But he'd also been fooling himself with his altruism when, honestly, he just wanted to spend time with her. Find out if he could trust her. See who she really was behind the perfect makeup and fancy clothes.

"I'm sorry I overreact and I'm so mistrusting, cynical even. It's just that, I'm coming from a place where I wasn't used to kindness. For a long time. My husband made me feel invisible."

And now he wanted to reach into her past and punch her ex in the face for being mean to her. How could anyone ignore Alyson?

"So." She put on a happy face, and they continued walking. "No matter what I make from this sale, I'm really glad I came. Your family is absolutely wonderful. I'm more myself again. And, you're right. I needed a break. I'm sorry I was such a jerk. And thank you for looking out for me."

"Yeah. Of course. Anytime." *Ugh!* He sounded so lame. He was totally blowing this. He had to figure things out before she left. Once she did, they might never see each other again.

If he got the courage to ask her out now and she said no, would they even stay friends? He wasn't sure he wanted to risk that. Better friends than nothing. He could do something now and risk losing everything or do nothing and still have a chance someday.

Someday. A day that might never come, like his Hollywood dreams.

He watched her play with the ducks, attracting them by throwing leaves into the water. They waddled onto shore, much to her delight. She talked to them like they were people, apologizing for not having anything to feed them. So cute.

Other people approached, breaking the illusion of privacy in their cave of branches. Alyson said goodbye to the ducks, then surprised him by taking his arm at the elbow, leading him back the way they had come, away from the people. A good sign—she wanted to be alone with him too. He'd get another chance to say what he needed to say.

"Your Dad wasn't what I expected."

"No?"

"I expected him to be stern. But he's a sweetie like you, just . . . distracted."

Marcus laughed. "I'm not telling him that. 'Hey, Dad, you ol' wacky professor type.'" He chuckled. "Even if it's true, I'm not saying it."

"He didn't react to my being Catholic, but your sisters did. What's up with that?"

"Oh, that's nothing. Gail's ex was Catholic, and they disagreed on how to raise their kids. Turned out they disagreed on most everything. He wasn't a *bad* guy. Troubled is a better word." He recalled Gail's tearful cries into his mother's shoulder a few years ago, sobbing about his addiction relapse. His addiction to pornography. And Gail refused to raise children in such a house. "But that's for Gail to share with you someday."

"She did, a little. Just not the specifics. She told me they'd dated forever before getting married. Dated longer than they stayed married. What did your dad think?" She veered off the path and tugged him toward a bench.

Good. He didn't want to go back yet either. "What do you mean?"

"Did he approve of her marrying outside your faith? Living in sin? My father would've been . . . displeased . . . if he'd been alive when I married. My ex was not a spiritual man."

She met his gaze but then looked away, her neck and the tips of her ears reddening. "We'd lived together more than a year before Darius caused us to get married quicker than we'd planned." She offered a smile, feigning a nonchalance she couldn't keep up. "Actually, we hadn't thought that far into the future. Getting married was more a knee-jerk reaction than a plan."

Tingles blossomed below Marcus's ribs, that same sensation he'd experienced when he first knew God meant for him to help her. He didn't want to blow it by saying the wrong thing now she was opening up. But that was a lot to unpack. He took a deep breath, trying to breathe in God's wisdom. No words came. Instead, in the quiet, he sensed the guilt and shame covering her like a well-worn blanket. A blanket she clutched onto.

"Alyson." He softened his tone, so she would know he meant every word. "What the many books of the Bible and the writings of the church fathers and mothers, what *everything* boils down to is this: God loves you and wants a relationship with you, His creation. And there is *nothing* you can do to change His mind. Nothing."

She continued staring off across the open field instead of looking at him, but he noticed goosebumps had risen on her arms. What he'd said had hit home.

"So . . . your dad wasn't mad at Gail?"

"I'd say disappointed, not mad."

"She wasn't kicked out of the church?"

"What? No. Of course not." He looked at her anew. What had she experienced? "Everybody is a sinner. Kicking sinners out of the church would make it empty. Dad even tried to counsel John, Gail's ex, after they broke up. But John left anyway. And that tore Dad up because he knew John wouldn't step foot in church again."

They sat in silence. He followed her gaze and saw she observed a young family across the park, walking their dogs. A man and woman hand in hand, an older child holding the leashes of three mixed-breed dogs, a little girl with pig-tails running ahead.

"What if *I* never step foot in church again?" She said the words while looking away, but at the end, turned to him, her eyes challenging.

This was a test of some kind, but it didn't change his answer. "Dad preaches that God doesn't care where you go to church, just that you go. That you gather together to worship. Even in a friend's living room, if that's what feels right to you. God wants you to love and serve Him by loving and serving those He puts in your path. It's that simple. The rest is details."

She sighed. "Yes, people love to squabble over details." She watched the young family again. "Every church I've tried since I left home was destroying itself from the inside. Some of the most hateful, judgmental people I've met have called themselves Christians. It got to the point I didn't want to associate with people like that and stopped trying."

"But Darius didn't think twice before kneeling and praying that first night in the boys' bunk room. Not shy at all about talking to God. That's good Christian parenting."

"Well. I had to give him a foundation, an introduction. He wouldn't get it from anywhere else in his life. I was lucky I'd been steeped in it when I was young." She sighed. "But everything has changed."

"What do you mean?" He turned his body to better face her, though she continued to stay focused on the family across the field, the man and boy now playing frisbee keep-away with the dogs while the woman and young girl watched and clapped when a dog leaped for an interception.

"When I first moved back home, I had questions and needed someone to talk to who wouldn't fight with me like Mom or cry and pray for me like Luisa. I went back to the church where I grew up. But none of the same priests remained, none of the people remembered me, and I remembered no one. So many new buildings, everything modern, unrecognizable. Even the prayers had changed. I felt like a stranger."

"That's good that—"

"I mean, why did the *prayers* have to change? Were they *wrong*? I get the new buildings, but the beauty, the wonder and mystery were gone. It was as cold and clean as an IKEA store." Her ire incited her hands to do half the talking. "The people sang modern hymns instead of the amazing choir that gave me chills when I was a girl because it was so beautiful, so ethereal. So much for majesty. I mean, I might as well have walked into a Protestant church. There was nothing there for me." She glanced at him apologetically then, her fingertips brushing his arm. "No offense."

"It's all right." He could hear the grin in his voice and tried to make up for it by taking the hand that had touched him, but she pulled it away too soon, crossing her arms like she was cold. He didn't know what to make of all she'd said, but he loved that she allowed him a glimpse of her true self again. She trusted him. It was a start.

"So, soon I will have no home. And I already have no spiritual home. I'm leading my children into a kind of hell—" She turned away from him and took a ragged breath. "Uhg! I promised myself I'd stop doing this." She wiped her eyes, still facing away from him. "So embarrassing to be a leaky faucet all the time. I'm sorry. I'm not like this normally, I swear."

"You can find a new spiritual home, Alyson. And you can still give your sons a great childhood even if it isn't like the one you experienced."

She nodded and took another deep breath.

"Will you pray with me?" He put his hands out, palms up, expecting her to place her own in his.

She faced him with a *don't-be-stupid* look on her face. "Prayer doesn't work. Not for me. Didn't save my dad, didn't save my marriage, didn't help me one bit. I'm done. Besides, God washed his hands of me when I divorced, so I wash my hands of Him."

Stunned, Marcus couldn't even take a breath until the moment passed. He sat back, the wood slats of the bench hitting him in all the wrong spots. He had to tread softly now or risk pushing her further away.

She crossed her arms with a huff, but as the seconds ticked by the fight went out of her. She pressed her lips together as if afraid she would say more. Her eyes welled up once again, but she lifted her chin.

He had to admire her moxie. To be angry with God was to experience Him deeply. Most people didn't get that. You're *supposed* to wrestle with God, like Jacob.

Clearly, she was not done with God, and God was not done with her. God had put her here with

Marcus and his family to help right her heart. Marcus had to take his own desires out of the picture and simply be a conduit. Help God heal her soul.

What did she need? What had she said that he'd missed? He took a deep breath again and, eyes closed, remembered her saying she had questions.

"Why do you think God 'washed his hands of you'? Did you not get the answers you were looking for when you went back to your old church?"

"No. I asked a very specific question and instead of answering, *Father Coward* invited me to join a divorce support group that meets there." Her eyes narrowed with the memory. "I could've punched him. So dismissive."

"Well, try asking me."

The surprise in her big brown eyes edged on fear.

"I mean, I'm no Bible expert, but—"

"No, I think you're too close to the issue. I mean, for me, you're too close." Her gaze fell to chest-level as if she suddenly thought he was physically too close as well. "It's nice having a friend, I don't want to ruin that."

"Alyson, you can trust me. I only want what's best for you." He took her hand in his.

She pulled her hand back like it burned. "No, Marcus, that's just the trouble." She stood and walked a few steps away. He was about to follow when she turned back and pronounced, "Matthew 5:32: 'Anyone who divorces his wife, except on the grounds of sexual immorality, causes her to commit adultery, and anyone who marries a divorced woman commits adultery.' And those are red-letter words, Marcus. From Jesus Himself."

She paced on the crushed granite path. "So I am literally unlovable. For the rest of my life. Why would God do that to me?" Her voice trembled with anger and tears. "I didn't ask for any of this. I didn't have affairs.

"I tried to be a good wife. I tried to make him happy. I tried to save our stupid, horrible marriage, year after year. And he gets to just send me away, and I'm an adulteress if I fall in love again? How is that fair? And worse, if someone falls in love with me, I make him an adulterer?"

She came back and sat on the far side of the bench, cross-legged, half turned toward him. "I can't be with anyone ever again. I have to be alone or cause others to fall. God hates divorce, so God hates me."

He gave her a moment to calm down. Then he simply said, "No."

"No? What do you mean, no?"

"You're wrong. Flat out wrong."

Her stunned frozen features said she'd not expected disagreement. Pity, maybe. Sympathy, sure. Blame and shame, most definitely. But not relief.

"Again, I'm no expert, but I've learned a thing or two from Dad, and one of them is to always look at the context." He had her attention now, those intense eyes of hers bored into his own.

"Listen. Jesus was getting after people for being legalistic, for hiding behind the law instead of living from love and compassion." Marcus shifted toward her, seeing she was receptive. "He was telling guys they shouldn't just divorce their wives whenever they wanted—even though it was legal—because in that day and age, the culturally acceptable reason for divorce was infidelity.

"So if a man divorced his wife, for whatever reason, the society they lived in would assume there was infidelity on *her* part. And society was pretty darn tough on women anyhow, much less a woman who fell short. They would see a divorced woman and anyone she married afterward as *unclean* and shun them, even if they'd done no wrong." He let that sink in.

Her gaze had turned inward, her brow wrinkled.

"You see, Jesus was telling guys to man up and remember their commitments, not be fickle just because the law allowed it. No matter what, a man is to love his bride like God loves the church. Protect her. Build her up. Take care of her. Lay down his life for her."

She met his gaze then, with such a mix of sorrow and hope he felt it in his chest. But then she looked away, pulled her arms in tight across her chest, her hand over her mouth, and sat still for a long time.

He couldn't read her features, only knew that she was mulling things over.

He prayed that he'd helped and hoped the long silence was a good thing. He could wait.

Glancing out across the park again, he searched for the family with dogs. They were leaving, going back the way they had come, man and wife hand in hand, the little girl turning around to face them with arms up, wanting to be picked up by Daddy.

A simple moment. A pang of loneliness Marcus pushed away.

"You know what I think?"

He turned back to Alyson, hoping his thoughts hadn't shown on his face. "What?"

"That lasagna's not going to make itself." She slapped her thighs and stood, taking a deep breath. "I bet your uncle thinks we stole his car." She smiled for real this time. Her telltale eyes bright and playful again. She seemed happy as if none of the heaviness had ever happened.

What had changed in her?

They walked toward the car slowly, her hand on his arm, taking in the beautiful day. Whatever he'd said, whatever she'd heard, she was glowing.

He felt it too. Now that Alyson was happy, the sky was bluer, the clouds whiter, the grass greener than before. "So what happens when we get back to San Antonio?"

She smiled up at him, eyes twinkling. "I don't know. What do you want to happen?"

"Try again. I want you to try again to find a church family, a community you can grow in. One that will lift you when you get low. That's what it's all about. Loving your neighbor as yourself. And your neighbor is anyone God puts on your path. Like He put you on mine."

Her hand stiffened and slipped away.

He'd gone too far, pushed too hard. He could kick himself.

She lowered her head, her hands in pockets as they walked.

When she raised her head, she wore a closed-lip smile that wasn't fooling anybody. Her glow had vanished, replaced by a tightness. A formality. "Well, then. Thank you for lifting up the boys and me this Christmas. I'm glad we were in your path. You've been very kind."

Kind. Even kindness can be cruel.

Aww, come on! He'd done the right thing. He'd stepped back and risked their fledgling relationship to talk about God. He wasn't leading her on, he was trying to help. If he was leading anyone on, it was himself.

They continued toward the car, but now they were their own planets in their own orbits. If only he could take back what he'd said. If they could start over, they'd never leave the cave of willow branches.

He didn't want their time alone to end this way. "So what's next? When you get the money, have you decided what you'll do with it? Law school?"

She shook her head again. "No, law school feels angry. I'm so tired of being angry. It's the only thing that's been holding me up for months, but I can't do it anymore, I don't *want* to do it anymore.

"If I've learned anything from being around you and your family, it's that I want more joy. I don't want to always look at the past with hate and anger, I want to leave it there and" —she stopped, and he stopped with her— "make a fresh start." She paused, glancing in his eyes. Shook her head and sighed.

She walked forward again, holding her arms as if hugging herself. "I don't know. I'll finish my business degree, I guess. Maybe I can be an administrative assistant or something. At least I'd have a schedule that better matches the school day."

He hadn't meant to depress her, but her voice had taken on a melancholy tone despite the words. Something else was going on with her he wasn't privy to.

He'd better ask outright while he still had time but be careful not to push too hard. "We'll still be friends, right? When we get back to San Antonio?"

She took a long time to answer, and he guessed she was choosing her words to let him down easy.

"Yeah." She offered a closed-lip smile. An easy one this time. "Friends it is."

"Good. I'd like that." He gave her a quick sideways hug when they stopped at the car, relieved he would have another chance to see where this was going. "Hey. Did you bring a grocery list for the lasagna?"

She tapped her temple. "It's all right here."

He moved to open her door for her, but she rushed there first. "Got it, thanks." She slid into the seat without looking at him.

He noted something had definitely changed between them—they'd shared so much, she'd allowed him to see the true vulnerable Alyson, yet now she blocked him out, pushed him away.

He gathered himself into the passenger seat all too aware of the heavy mood that surrounded them.

She focused on driving, and he directed her back to the highway.

Brightening his tone in an attempt to lead them out of this funk and back to fun, he said, "Most folks have left but we've still got to feed fifteen people. Think we can do it? I mean, I know *I* could, it's *you* I'm worried about. Cracking under the pressure and all."

She waggled her finger in his face, smiling with the challenge, playing along. "Ha! You're going down, mister! I make the *best* lasagna. You'll see."

He returned the smile but couldn't help feeling like something was missing now. They were both trying too hard to lighten the mood.

He turned on the radio to drown out the thoughts plaguing him. Once she finished the paperwork on the car, she wouldn't need him in her life anymore. The distance between them—she was already leaving.

Chapter Sixteen

Alyson and Marcus set the groceries on Mama Dottie's now immaculate counters.

"Is it time? Is it time?" Darius zoomed into the kitchen.

"Give me thirty minutes." Alyson removed her too-warm cardigan, preparing to cook. "I'll call you in when it's time to layer everything, okay?" She unpacked the groceries, setting the onions and peppers next to the cutting board for Marcus.

"Promise?" Darius bunched up his face.

"Cross my heart. No backsies." Alyson drew an X over her heart with a finger then held both hands up, fingers wide.

Darius smiled and skipped away to rejoin his friends.

"Okay, we have a pan for the meat, but where—"

"Wait. First things first. I've got to get tunes playing. Any requests?"

"Yeah, no lyrics or we won't be able to chat."

He saluted casually and walked out.

She'd expected him to start a playlist on his phone, but she was glad to have a moment to herself. With a puffed-cheek exhale, she rounded and relaxed her shoulders for the first time in hours. She tensed when he touched her and tensed when she expected his touch and didn't receive it. Now she was nothing but tense muscles all over. A hot bath was what she needed. Instead, she was cooking for fifteen.

"Need any help?" Gail stood in the doorway.

"Does your mom have a lasagna pan? Any large, deep casserole dish will do, I guess."

Gail stepped in to show her. Bending down to the low cupboard, she pulled out two glass dishes, handing one to Alyson. "Can you show me where Marcus's YouTube channel is again? I tried to find it but forgot that stupid stage name of his."

"Marcus Kafele." Marcus's tone simmered with anger.

Alyson almost dropped the glass casserole dish.

He stood in the doorway, a CD-player in hand. "It means 'He who would die for you.' It's to center me." He glared at Gail. "No wisecracks? You're losing your touch."

"I'm sorry, Marcus," Alyson interrupted, hating the conflict between them. "It's my fault. I should never have brought it up."

Gail took her phone from her back pocket. "How do you spell that? Ka-what?"

"Get out, Gail. Go away."

"Hey, someone had to help her get started. Where were you?" But she was already walking past him and into the hall as she said it.

"I'm so sorry." Alyson hadn't realized it would make him so upset to share his music with his family.

He stepped closer and set the CD-player on the counter. "Bound to happen eventually. How did you find me, anyway?"

The ability to lie easily would've been much appreciated right now. "Um … I kind of kept scrolling through different musicians named Marcus until I … sort of … you know, recognized your hands."

A slow, knowing smile took over his mouth, alighted in his eyes. "How many did you go through?"

"Oh, not too many." Right. It had only taken an entire afternoon. She busied herself with unpacking the meat and getting ready to brown it. Her face and ears were on fire. Luckily, he busied himself with the CDs and player. She didn't think she could withstand any teasing, her heart was already so wounded and raw.

On the bench in the park, she had almost blurted out her feelings for him and had to cover her mouth to hold it inside. She'd actually prayed then: *God help me, I'm afraid I love this man.*

But Marcus didn't want her. He felt deeply, yes, but not about her.

When he spoke of love and commitment and how a man was to love his bride, she'd hoped there was something between them, that he felt it too.

But then when she looked into his eyes and said she wanted to make a fresh start, subtext: with you! He didn't get it. Which meant she was fooling herself.

What did she expect? They barely knew each other.

Friends was good enough.

Wasn't it?

"Ready for great tunes?" Marcus was smiling again. "This is my gramps and his band. His last album. He's the oboe and clarinet. Arthritis got too bad after this."

A soulful cover of "Stormy Weather" played. Marcus turned it up.

While she browned the meat, she swayed and sang along with the oboe, doing Ella Fitzgerald's part.

Determined not to spend the last night of her vacation in another silly drama of her own making, she silently vowed to keep things as light and friendly as possible.

And yet, she was only too aware that Marcus rarely took his dreamy gaze off of her as she sang the old torch song.

He really seemed into her, seemed to enjoy being with her, so why didn't he make a move? Despite what he'd said in the park about what God thought of divorce, she was still damaged goods. She cringed, remembering how he'd said God put her on his path—to be a charity case. Like anyone else he might help on his path. Sure, Marcus was attracted to her, and she to him, but they both knew she had nothing to offer anyone but a bunch of broken pieces.

Stop it, Stefanelli. Enough. Enjoy this last night.

She took a deep breath and sang about walking in the sun like she actually believed it was possible. But then the lyrics about a love who left her stopped her cold—it was too close to home.

And yet, her own stormy weather had nothing to do with the man who left her, not anymore, but with the man in front of her.

She had tonight. Only tonight. Her life would be back to overwork and overwhelm as soon as she got back to San Antonio.

Marcus handed her the cutting board full of chopped onion. "What else can I do?"

She slid them into the huge skillet of meat and stirred as a new song played. "Can you waltz?"

"Excuse me?"

"This song is a waltz." She demonstrated the classic box step, counting aloud, "One-two-three, two-two-three." She held her arms up, waiting for him to join her on their makeshift dance floor.

"I'm not a dancer." And yet he grasped her raised hand in his and put his other hand on her hip. She smiled at the too-intimate touch and the sudden intensity in his eyes but moved his hand up. "Your hand goes on my shoulder blade. My arm rests on yours."

"Oh. Sorry." He looked embarrassed. "I told you I'm no dancer."

"That's all right, I'm no musician." She pulled him into the box step slowly. Once, twice . . .

"But we both feel the music."

She glanced to his eyes to see how he meant what he'd said, but he watched his feet.

"I've never danced a waltz in my life. How did you do that? I'm dancing."

"Don't look down. Let the music lead your feet. Ready to travel?"

"Travel?"

"Watch me." She broke from him and danced a flowing box step with an imaginary partner until she made a circle. "You use pressure in your hands to tell me where we're going, and I follow, okay?"

"Am I ready for that? This is my first lesson."

"You're a man. A man leads." She smiled and raised her brow in challenge.

He opened his mouth but said nothing. Instead, a new fire lit his eyes, his lips curling. He took her in his arms once more.

She had tonight.

Chapter Seventeen

"Dinner is served," Alyson and Marcus said in unison, and each placed a casserole dish of lasagna on the table before the seated family members. Marcus had the energy to do sprints after playing around in the kitchen with Alyson—such a shame that the food was ready.

Kids ran in from the other room and sat at a folding table. Darius peeked at the grown-ups' table and announced, "Marcus wins! He put pepperoni in his!"

Marcus stood aside, his hand on the small of Alyson's back. "Hey, hey, now. In all fairness, it's your mom's recipe for both of them. I just added my favorite pizza toppings. So, we have a nice classic meat and cheese lasagna from Alyson . . ." He paused a moment to perform a soft golf-clap.

"And on my side, we have a Grade-A, super-powered, locked-and-loaded, over-the-top, slap-your-mama-it's-so-good, king lasagna." The boys cheered their hero.

Alyson laughed and smacked his arm playfully.

He tugged her closer for a friendly side hug—which they'd done before—but she stiffened. Why?

She stepped away from him and began serving the lasagna, her glance to him something between an apology and regret.

If only he knew which it was.

In the car, they had sung at the top of their lungs to an old 90s grunge song they both liked. At the grocery store, they'd acted like kids, her standing on the edge of the shopping cart and him pushing too fast, making her squeal. Saying out loud that they would continue being friends had seemed to free Alyson to be herself more, to loosen up.

Like their fight, what happened at the park released pressure, allowed him to peel away the layers that separated them. Little by little, he grew closer to the real Alyson.

He wanted to peel away her tough outer layers.

They'd danced together in the kitchen as much as they'd cooked. If they cooked like that all the time, he had a feeling a lot of meals would get burned. He didn't think 'just friends' would last long. At least, he hoped not.

But now she's pulling away again. Why?

They were on the edge of something, a wave about to crest.

Or maybe it was all wishful thinking.

"Well, Marcus?" Mama said. "Aren't you going to help, or is poor Alyson serving yours too?"

"Oh, no. I don't dare." Alyson smirked. "His royal lasagna is waaaay too much for me to handle."

"Oooo! You hear that?" Gail said to Marianne.

"I do believe that was a *burn*." Marianne smiled at him, then blew him a kiss. Marianne had been too sweet to Alyson and him today. What had put her in such a good mood?

He got into the game and helped serve.

Once they were seated, with salad and garlic bread on the table, they all joined hands, and Marcus's dad said a short blessing. Marcus was about to let go of Alyson's and Marianne's hands at the end of the familiar blessing, when his father added, "And thank you, Jesus, for new friends You bring into our lives to wake us up and help see You anew. Amen."

Marcus squeezed Alyson's hand, and she squeezed back. He hazarded a glance only to meet her warmly smiling eyes.

He smiled back, his father's words ringing true deep inside him.

But the shadow of that thought darkened his view—what if Alyson wasn't attracted to him at all, but attracted to the kindness and joy she felt here? She wanted more joy. That didn't mean she wanted him.

Maybe he should be more focused on helping her back into God's arms rather than leading her into his own. Had their talk in the park had any effect?

He sighed. What was right?

He tried to join the conversation but wandered back to remembering the feel of Alyson in his arms as they danced. He could twirl her all night long if she'd let him.

When he had come up behind her at the sink as she was washing her hands and he'd washed his right on top of hers—it had been playful, silly at first, but it had also trapped her inside his arms. And that's when he knew in his heart, his dad was right. He'd led her on.

He wanted her, and he'd moved too fast without even realizing it. He knew he wasn't staying—he would leave for L.A. as soon as he could—yet he kept toying with Alyson. He wasn't being fair to her. Or himself.

Maybe it was a good thing their time together was ending soon. He needed to clear his head and focus on what was next in his plan. Rework his financials, search for impressive gigs.

"Marcus. I'm talking to you," Marianne said.

He pulled out of his thoughts to hear Marianne, Gail and Mama laughing at him. Alyson and Dad looked down at their plates.

"What did you say?"

"You're twenty-eight, when are you going to start thinking about starting a family?"

Dumbstruck. That was the kind of question girls were asked.

"Don't you want one?" Gail added.

"Of course. But I haven't accomplished anything yet."

"There's no hurry, baby. It's just that your dad and I aren't getting any younger."

"What? Why—"

Alyson put her hand on his, stopping him from arguing. "Marcus is on his way to Hollywood to write movie scores."

The silence around the table kept Marcus's gaze on his plate. He couldn't stomach seeing their reactions to his dream.

"Marcus, right now, your choices are as wide as the horizon," Alyson continued. "Your life is as flexible as you want it to be. Adding kids makes things very concrete, it narrows your choices, and takes your energy. You don't want to spend your days worrying about daycare and fevers and potty-training. You can still chase your dream."

"Alyson—" He tried to stop her.

"No, I'm serious. You need to stop trying to help everyone—the school, the kids, the studio, the local theater, *me*. Do what's going to get you closer to your goal while you still can. Make contacts now. Get a manager. You know I'm right."

He glanced at his mom and dad but couldn't read their expressions. He couldn't believe she was doing this in front of his family.

"Marcus." She pulled his shoulder to get him to face her and met his gaze dead on, like no one else was in the room. "You are *brilliant*. And anyone who works with you will see that. Stop selling yourself short. You're just postponing your success. You don't know how amazing you are. You don't see how people respond to you."

His anger melted away as he stared into her pleading eyes.

"It's true, son."

Why was Dad getting involved in this?

His father put his fork down. "I've seen the same thing. I've been meaning to talk with you about your options—"

"Can we talk about something besides me? I'm being pushed and pulled here."

"We could talk about your ego," Gail offered. "It's so big. Such substance."

"No one's pushing you away, honey." Mama seemed worried. Again.

He watched Alyson who stared at her half-eaten plate of food. She'd eaten more of the lasagna he'd made than her own. A little while ago they'd been laughing in the kitchen. This day had started out so awesome, and now it had fallen apart. Why? Why couldn't they just stay happy?

Alyson looked up and met his gaze with such large sorrowful eyes, eyes that did more than apologize. She felt responsible for his outburst. How could she push him away so hard when every look she gave him said she wanted him closer?

"Why don't you and Alyson take the kids in the family room and watch a movie while we clean up? His mom looked at both of them in turn.

The kids heard this and zoomed out of the room with shouts of glee.

"I'll clean. I made the mess, so I should clean it up." Alyson was already on her feet taking up the finished plates. "I'm a pretty messy cook. Why use one bowl when four will do?" She laughed.

He knew her well enough now to know she was trying to cover. Either she was playing at being perfect because she still thought she had to earn their hospitality or she would rather clean than talk to him.

"No, dear. You and Marcus made supper, so y'all go relax while we clean up. This'll be the first time all day I've done anything in my own kitchen thanks to all you kids." She patted both of them toward the door, shooing them out together. Literally pushing them together—he crashed into and almost tripped over Alyson. He looked back at his mom, and she smiled a big Cheshire Cat grin.

He shook his head, still smiling at his mom, the not-so-smooth matchmaker.

"Sorry. You first." He guided Alyson with a hand at her back, shifted it to her shoulder, then broke contact completely. What was this addiction to touching her, anyway?

When they were alone in the hallway, with kitchen noises on one side and children voting on what movie to watch on the other, she stopped him and, only inches away, looked up to him. "You know I had to do all that, right? They needed to hear you play. They need to know what drives you. You shouldn't hide from those you love. Those who love you."

As angry and embarrassed as he'd been a few minutes before, right now he wanted nothing more than to kiss her. He fought the urge.

Then, just as he changed his mind, she walked away.

He blew out his breath like he'd been punched in the gut.

"Have we chosen a movie?"

He could hear the kids and her perky voice but couldn't see any of them, couldn't be seen. Maybe he should cool it and go be by himself a while. Get some distance.

"Yeah! We voted fair and square," Moses answered. "It's *Shrek*."

"*Shrek*? My favorite! *What are you doing in my swamp!*" She said the last in a dead-on imitation of Mike Myers as the big green ogre himself. The kids roared.

Any thoughts of being alone flew from Marcus's head. He *had* to see this, especially if she was doing impressions.

She kept it up for the first part as she and Darius entertained them with the dialogue between Shrek and Donkey. She was so fun and open and silly. He loved it. Loved how relaxed she got when she was around the kids.

Darius sat between them on the couch when reciting Donkey's best lines, but he soon moved to be with the other boys on the floor.

Then Andre fell asleep in her arms, and she put him on a blanket next to her, scooting closer to Marcus to make room for her big toddler.

Marcus spent the next fifteen minutes intensely aware of how her body touched his all along the side. He tried not to move, even though he would be more comfortable putting his arm behind her, but then she might think he was trying to make a move. Just casual. Just friends.

She giggled at the movie and looked up at him to see if he laughed too. He smiled back, pretending he'd been paying attention. The change in her warmed his heart. He had respected her as a boss but had felt how her business-like demeanor masked her true self. It wasn't natural for her. *This* was the real Alyson. She wasn't trying to control everything, she wasn't trying to be perfect, she was just enjoying the moment. He wanted to take away her worries, so she could enjoy *every* moment.

Whole scenes of the movie flew by, the kids laughing while he tried to figure out what he would say if she called him on how close they were. Eventually, he relaxed enough to enjoy the movie. But at that point he felt her slump against him, asleep. He smiled at his worry. She was obviously comfortable enough with their closeness. Comfortable enough to sleep.

He took a deep breath and relaxed, then shifted slowly, gently, putting his arm around her and settling her against his chest. And he was caught in a realization so strong and so pure that it was a physical pain in his heart—he wanted this life. Not his current life of living alone and eating takeout, but this life, this pretend life. A beautiful, smart, funny, courageous woman in his arms, a room full of happy children, full-bellied from a big meal they'd made together. Everyone warmed by the fire, smiling and relaxed. A perfect moment.

But the ache in his chest grew as he remembered his father's warning—*don't be selfish. She's hurting. Be sure what you want. Don't lead her on. Even kindness can be cruel.*

Did he want her? Or did he want this dream? Was he being fair to her? Or was he using her to not feel so lonely? To pretend at least one part of his life was a success already. That felt true too, and it hadn't even occurred to him until now.

His favorite student was like a son to him. And the beautiful mother needing his help . . . He'd given in to the fantasy.

It bothered him that he could not tease apart his own motivations. He so often acted on impulse, or what felt right in his gut, in his heart. But what felt right to him could hurt her. For once, he didn't know if he could trust his feelings.

She shifted, pulling her bare feet up under her, burrowing into him for warmth. No blanket in sight, he pulled her closer, breathing in her flowery scent.

He knew what he *should* do. He should wake her up, so she and Andre could sleep in the comfortable bed. He *should* keep this casual and friendly and not wish for things that were not his. He *should* trust God and God's timeline for his life, and not try to force it by taking advantage of the beautiful, vulnerable, young mother just so he could pretend he had the family he always thought he'd have by now.

His sigh came out in ragged chunks, full of self-loathing.

He shook her gently with the arm that surrounded her, supported her. "Alyson. Wake up."

She shifted, sleepily sighed and steadied herself by moving her arm.

Her hand landed in the hollow of his chest, right where he ached and felt the shame of his selfishness.

"Alyson." He jostled her a little more.

"Marcus." Darius stood before him, a juice box in his hand. He must've seen them when coming back from the kitchen. The other kids were still in front of the TV, though the two girls turned around at hearing someone speak.

Marcus tried to sit up straighter, but the generous leather couch and Alyson's weight against him made it impossible. "What is it, buddy? Need help with the straw?" He held out his free hand.

Darius shook his head with a smile. "Are you going to be my daddy now?"

Oh no. What had he done? He pulled free the arm supporting Alyson, but it only made her lean into him more—almost in his lap now. She stirred, but nestled back against his chest with a low moan.

"No, Darius. Your mom and I are just friends. You know that, right?"

"But . . ." His brow pulled down in a confused scowl. He pointed to where his mom still nestled against Marcus's chest. "You're sleeping together."

"No!" Marcus sat straight up. Alyson, roughly jostled, startled awake. "Darius. You can't say that. It doesn't mean what you think it means."

His two nieces giggled. Great. An audience.

"But my friend Tommy, you know, from school? His parents aren't married, they just sleep together. That's what you guys—"

"No, Darius. That's *not* what's going on here. Your mom and I are just friends. That's it." He hadn't meant to sound gruff, but his tone left no room for comment.

"Oh boy." Alyson pressed against her eyes, ran her fingers through her hair, and then pulled it as if she were pulling out the tiredness. "Darius, love, come help me put Andre to bed, please."

"But Mom, it's only eight o'clock—"

"You've seen this movie a hundred times. And it sounds like we need to have a talk." She scooped up Andre from the other side of the couch.

"Sorry," Marcus said lamely.

"No, this is my fault. I'm sorry." But she didn't even look at him.

Andre didn't awaken, but he fisted his little hands and settled against her shoulder, his soft sleepy face a vision of complete trust and surrender.

Like she had nestled against his shoulder. He could still feel the heat of her there. Caring for another, wanting trust and surrender from another. Why would God put these strong feelings in him only to deny him a family?

Alyson walked past Darius and said, "Come along." Darius glowered. But when his gaze met Marcus's, he changed from a glower to a frown as if Marcus had rejected *him*, not his idea.

In a way, he had. Marcus wished he could redo the whole thing.

"Darius, don't make me ask again, sweetheart." Her tone was kind but firm. Darius went, putting his hand in hers and looking over his shoulder at Marcus.

What had he done?

He wanted to fix things with Darius. He wanted to help her explain things to him, to make things right. But it wasn't his place. He was not the boy's father. He was no one's father. No one's husband. He rubbed his temples, then his face.

He'd had the chance to do the right thing, and instead acted selfishly—he'd *wanted* her in his arms. Now, Darius was confused, and Alyson had a difficult, touchy situation ahead of her.

It was obvious why God held back—Marcus was still such a child, unable to put others before himself.

His lack of impulse control had almost had him marrying Yvonne when they'd had so little in common—just because he wanted to hurry up and be married. She had toyed with him, led him astray. Thank God she'd left him when she did.

Or maybe, God held back because a family would distract him from his goals, his calling.

Maybe bringing Alyson here for Christmas had been a selfish act after all. Maybe he shouldn't have invited her. Maybe he shouldn't have gotten involved with the Santa crisis at the mall. Even his helping had been a selfish act. The crowd had loved him.

What was selfish? What was self-less?

He didn't trust any of his motivations anymore. He should never have brought her here.

৵৵

Alyson didn't come out of the room again until Darius, too, was asleep—after almost two hours of talking and playing games, just the two of them like it would've been at home. She hoped he understood everything she'd told him. It was hard knowing what he could understand and what was too advanced, too grown-up for him to hear.

Even so, after hearing Marcus repeat "just friends" so adamantly, she thought it best they go back to a more formal routine. Both of them.

Just friends. She and Marcus had been getting closer the past few days. Sure it was always two steps forward and one step back, but still, they definitely had a bond. She'd begun to think that maybe he had invited them because he really did want her to meet his family and get to know him better. Guess not. She had read him wrong yet again.

In every situation—in the park, in the kitchen, every time she thought he might be interested in her, he said something that threw her back to feeling like a stupid twit, seeing romance in situations where it plainly didn't exist. Wishful thinking. She was nothing but a desperate, foolish girl who needed to grow up and guard her heart.

Walls offer support after all. Distance offers objectivity. It didn't cancel out any of the great things he'd done for her, it just meant she wanted what she couldn't have. 'Just friends' was enough. It would have to be. It might even be too much.

The house was strangely quiet since it had been rowdy the last two nights at this time. But she was glad for some quiet, so she could make a few calls undisturbed.

She hoped her East Coast friends didn't mind the interruption. This early on a Saturday night, some of them were probably on their way to a party or out for after-dinner drinks. She dialed her old bestie from the dance studio. The once best friend she'd been too ashamed to call before now.

"Hi, Hee-Young, am I disturbing anything? It's Alyson Daniels."

"Alyson! What happened to you? Why haven't you called? You dropped off the face of the earth."

"Yeah, I've been busy trying to put my life back together. I promise to call again so we can catch up, but tonight I need a favor. If you don't mind. If you're busy, I can call back later."

"First of all, you don't have to sound so pathetic when asking for a favor. I owe you a *million* favors. Maybe two million. And second, what's with the Southern accent?"

Alyson laughed. It was such a relief to know she could pick up where she'd left off with at least one of her friends. She filled her in about Marcus, his talent, and his plans to go to L.A. soon. "Do you have any contacts, any at all, who could help?"

"Oh, sweet cherubic girl that you are. You *know* I have contacts. Even my corns and bunions have industry contacts. Send me some links so I can see what I'm dealing with here."

Marcus kept playing the same notes over and over on the old Sony keyboard in the garage. It was his warm-up, but he wasn't warming up, literally or figuratively. His breath came out in clouds. He shivered but kept at it until something more came to him. He closed his eyes and pictured Alyson.

In his memory, she stood there in his man cave, astounded by her son's ability to play the piano. The way she'd looked at him had taken his breath away. Marcus switched to "Hot Cross Buns," playing it classical-style, heavy on the baroque, and chuckled. She would like that silliness.

He prayed, just a whisper, "God, what is it she needs to hear? What is it I need to play?" As usual, feelings, thoughts, ideas started coming to him, and he played a bit, then grabbed the graph paper he'd brought in and started scribbling notes. Praying always opened him up, so why didn't he ever remember to start with prayer in the first place?

He tried on the keyboard what he'd just written, played it over and over, and words came—a conversation. He recorded it on the page, music and lyrics coming fast.

He worked in a fugue, no longer aware of the cold, until his phone rang. He fished it out of his pocket, then saw it was his dad calling.

"Hey, Dad."

"Where are you? I've been looking all over the house for you."

"In the garage. I'm writing. I'll be in soon—your office?"

"Yes." His dad ended the call.

Marcus didn't have a clue what his dad wanted to talk about but was glad he was still awake. He needed a talk to clear his mind, get back on a righteous path.

His desires, his selfishness, had him all confused.

He walked into his dad's study, almost as cold as the garage thanks to a partially open window—a quirk of his dad's. *Got to allow an opening for the Spirit to come in.* He wasn't superstitious. It was a metaphorical reminder he'd adopted since writing a book about the early monastic Christians of Egypt and Ethiopia. But it was cold. His dad didn't seem to notice. He put aside what he was working on, clearing the way for their conversation.

"Marcus. I know how you feel about *moving on*, but I want you to know your options." He raised his hands, palms stalling Marcus's objections before he could verbalize them. "Please hear me out. Your brother is great as associate pastor. But he approaches the Word intellectually. He says all the right things, yet doesn't connect well with the people. He lives too much with his head and not enough with his heart.

"Now you. You always connect. You live a Christ-centered, heart-centered life, always trying to help people, always reaching out—and that's *natural* for you, not an intellectual exercise, not a discipline. You and your brother are—"

"Opposites?" He offered without charity.

"—two sides of the same coin. And I need you *both*. You add a youthfulness, a joyfulness to the church we've been missing ever since you left. I've been getting texts from our members who were so happy to see you at the candlelight service. You're well-loved here. Why is Hollywood such a draw?"

"Dad, please don't. Please don't make me feel bad for wanting something else."

"I'm sorry. I promised your mother I'd steer clear and only make sure you knew your options. It's an associate pastorship, son. Not music director, not focused on the audio and video production. A real pastorship you can grow into. One you can make your own someday. Alyson is right. People respond to you in a way they just don't respond to others."

"Dad. I . . ." Marcus sighed and sat down in the guest chair. "I feel, deep down, that I've got to go. I've got to do this, Dad. I've got to try."

"Why haven't you made the leap? What holds you back?" Dad's inquisitive tone was also gentle.

Marcus had expected confrontation but instead was being ministered to.

"I need a few more big-name gigs I can use as references to help me get a foot in the door. That's the only reason I'm hesitating. Honest. It's not doubt." But saying it aloud he knew it wasn't the whole truth. As long as he held back, there was still hope. Once he was out there, he'd have to face reality.

"I just . . . I don't want to lose you, son. I feel like I'm losing you."

Marcus's breath caught in his throat, hollowed out by the idea he'd hurt his father. "No, Dad. Impossible." He crossed to his dad behind the leather-topped desk and hugged him.

At the feel of his slighter frame, Marcus realized that this offer wasn't just to get him to stay home. He held his dad at arm's length and noticed his hair was more white than black now. He had the same burning eyes and thick jaw, but more wrinkles than Marcus remembered.

Dad wasn't trying to get him to stay because he thought he couldn't make it on his own, he was trying to get him to stay because he wanted both his sons to inherit his legacy and the church he'd dedicated his life to.

Without Marcus, his dad might not be able to retire any time soon. But his dad wouldn't come out and say that. It would be too much pressure.

When they'd fought in July, Marcus had gotten mad at his father for guilting him into participating in the services whenever he was home. Requiring it, even, as if he were still a child who could be told what to do. Now it seemed clear his dad had been trying to test him, prepare him for taking over, for pastoring with his brother.

But his whole body screamed 'no!' at the thought.

"Dad, thank you for the offer. It means a lot to know you have faith in me to keep up the work you've started. But I don't—"

"Don't answer now." His dad patted Marcus's chest over his heart. "Think about it. Spend a year in California. Maybe two. Whatever you need. *Then* give me your answer. Okay? There's no deadline on this." His dad's fiery eyes pleaded with his own.

Then Dad smiled, breaking the spell. "And please be part of the services tomorrow, son. Everyone loves it when you do Children's Church, especially the children. You know how to reach them."

Marcus smiled knowingly. "Okay, Dad."

"And maybe sing in the choir?"

"You're pushing it."

Dad laughed. "I know. I know."

"I'll be part of services tomorrow if you'll let me do this song for Alyson at the end." He took his notes out of his pocket and handed them to his dad.

He read it over, but by the look on his face, couldn't understand much of it. "Are you sure? What is your aim with this song?"

"I don't know, but if life were a movie, this would be on her soundtrack. She needs to hear it. I need to play it."

His dad breathed out a long sigh. And another, like he was choosing not to say what he wanted to. "Okay. I'll trust you need to do this since you feel strongly about it. But there's no time to practice with the choir or an accompanist."

"I know. Just me and the piano. I hope it's enough."

Chapter Eighteen

"Well, good morning Darius, dear! Don't you look handsome in your suit."

Marcus turned at the mention of a suit. Sure enough, Darius was in a nice gray suit and purple tie. A nicer suit than Marcus owned.

"Good morning, Mrs. Powell. Thank you."

Mama looked at Marcus with some alarm and crossed the kitchen to Darius. "What's the matter, honey? You want some breakfast? Best oatmeal you've ever had, I guarantee it."

"Yes, please. Thank you." Darius took off his jacket and folded it on the back of the chair. He sat, head propped up on his fists, looking glum.

Marcus glanced at his mom, seeing her worried brow over being called 'Mrs. Powell' instead of 'Mama Dottie.' A ball of lead rolled in Marcus's gut. He went to check on Alyson and knocked on the bedroom door.

Alyson let him in. She was dressed in an outfit that belonged in an old movie—mid-calf length, belted, fitted perfectly to her frame, her hair tied back in the low chignon she wore at work. She didn't smile.

The ball of lead sank deeper. He was responsible. What he'd done last night—taking liberties—had caused her to close off again, just when he'd gotten her to open up.

He glanced around the room, wondering what to say. She'd cleaned—the room was in better shape now than when they'd arrived. Their bags were already packed. Andre was on the bed, kicking his legs, and, without a word, she went back to trying to get his socks and shoes on him.

"You're still coming to church with us, aren't you?"

"Yes, of course, that's why I'm dressed like this."

"Lots of people dress casually. Jeans are okay." He motioned to the jeans he was wearing.

She met his gaze, and he couldn't read what her eyes were telling him. "This is how I was raised. It's who I am."

"Hey, if dressing up is how you show respect to God, that's cool. No one's asking you to change."

Her eyes flicked to his, and then away. "Good. Because I'm not going to."

She seemed upset, and he had no idea why. "Are we still talking about clothes? If this has gone deeper, you've got to clue me in, because I'm lost."

She rolled her eyes, but a smile played at her lips. And yet she was trying to cover that smile as she finished putting Andre's shoes on him. He squirmed out of her grasp and began unpacking their travel toy box. She sat on the bed and sighed but let him be.

The longer Marcus let the silence grow, the more certain he was that she was trying to avoid looking at him.

"Hey, listen, I'm sorry about last night."

She waved it away like it didn't matter. "Don't be. Darius is fine."

He wanted to say, "It's you I'm worried about." But couldn't. His heart and throat burned with words unspoken. He hoped his song would change that. He only wanted the best for her. Instead of saying what was in his heart he filled the silence with, "I'm singing in church today."

"I figured you would, that's why I agreed to come." She still wouldn't look at him.

"I wrote the song for you."

He had her attention now. Her eyes bored into him. She seemed angry. Frowning, she turned away, her eyes focused on her packed luggage.

"Marcus." She said nothing more, but her tone conveyed that he had gone too far, that this was too much, that knowing he wrote a song for her angered or frustrated her.

He'd hoped it would please her. But at least she was coming. At least he had another chance to explain himself.

"I need to help set up, but there will be a caravan of folks going from the house to the church. You won't get lost."

"I won't get lost."

Her smile made him realize how his statement had sounded more like a question, more like he was worried she was going to take off first chance she got and not see him perform. But it didn't matter. At least she'd smiled.

Alyson had gotten lost. Not just when following Marianne, but then again by missing the turn-in because she was looking for a church and this looked like a conference center. She'd passed it twice. Then she couldn't find a parking spot, and a cop had directed her to a parking lot farther back. Who had cops directing traffic in a church parking lot?

A church like no other she had ever been in. Snazzy ultra-modern decor, with painted concrete floors, like walking on a mural. This wasn't cold, but artistic. She'd entered glass doors to come upon a welcome station called the "Shalom Center" and a sign that listed so many meeting rooms they'd run out of apostles and started naming them after other important people in the Bible. She couldn't get a grip on what denomination this was—it didn't seem to be stated anywhere. Nothing was what she'd expected.

"Ma'am? Are you looking for the childcare wing?" A pretty Asian woman with a pixie cut spoke to her from behind the Shalom Center counter. "You can drop them off now, or you can take them in with you. Either way is fine."

"Oh, okay. Thank you." She felt a little like Alyson in Wonderland. As she walked down the hallway toward the children's rooms, she smelled coffee and heard chatter. Closer still and she saw people sitting on couches and at bistro sets, drinking coffee and watching screens.

On screen, Marcus's brother, Lawrence, gave the week's announcements and reminders. Surreal. So far from her simple Catholic upbringing.

The boys were welcomed into their respective rooms and were happy to join in because they already had friends there—Marcus's younger nieces and nephews amidst lots of other little kids.

She grabbed some coffee and tried to appear nonchalant while she sipped and figured out where she was supposed to go next.

"Is this your first time here? You look a little lost." An older woman wearing a painted wooden rosary as a necklace approached her.

Alyson took the rosary as a sign. "Yes. Yes, I am a little lost."

"We're going in, come with us."

She tossed the half-drunk coffee in the bin and followed the trio of women down another hall.

"That's a beautiful rosary."

"Thank you, child. It was a graduation gift— older than you are. I carry it with me always." Smalltalk revealed the woman was a sister working as a social worker. The other two women were also social workers, but lay-people.

Alyson wanted to ask more questions, find out why the sister was there, but they had come to a door. A small, older gentleman, white handlebar mustache against coppery skin, opened the door for them, releasing the miked sound of Lawrence finishing up the announcements. She stepped into a darkened hallway.

When she turned the corner, her jaw dropped. Stadium seating, screens everywhere, a light show on a shimmering backdrop. No wonder Marcus saw Hollywood as attainable—he'd grown up in a theater. Church here was a big production.

One thing was still the same as in any church though—the back seats filled in first leaving only the ones in the front for latecomers like her.

Music started up and then singing. A jazzier version of the usual Christmas songs, a medley, running from the birth story right through to the visit by the Three Kings. She heard Marcus's voice among the singers—she'd recognize it anywhere—but she couldn't see him.

She walked down the long aisle and was stopped by someone with a headset who directed her to a row where seats were available. Not the kind of usher she was used to in a church. Finally, she got to an empty seat close enough to the aisle that she wouldn't have to crawl over people.

It was hard to think of this as a church with the comfortable padded individual seats and armrests. As a student, she had been used to sitting and kneeling on wood, the cushioned pews reserved for the elderly. No screens. No microphones.

She had forgotten to pick up a bulletin—if there was one—so didn't understand what was happening when. It seemed haphazard to her.

When Marcus's dad announced Marcus was there for Children's Church, she heard a wave of hushed, excited chatter from the women around her, young and old. It seemed they thought he was a pretty good catch, single too long. Alyson laughed to herself—women were perpetual matchmakers, no matter the denomination.

Another thing she noticed—the older women dressed up like she did, smart skirt suits or dresses, some with hats or a matching clutch. But those around her age dressed more casually, as Marcus had said. Not even thirty and she already fit in with the AARP crowd.

Marcus did cut a fine image on stage. Jeans with a blazer that made his shoulders seem even broader. He looked comfortable, though, like the stage was merely an extension of his living room. He called all the kids up to join him on the stage steps.

The kids from the childcare wing walked down the middle aisle in single file, but Darius started skipping and jumping up and down, climbing around other kids to get close to Marcus. They sat on the wide steps leading up to the stage and Marcus sat among them.

He small-talked with them about Christmas and presents and parties and guests for a minute. "Did you have any guests at your house? Or maybe you were a guest at someone else's house? Yeah? Did you have to *do* anything to *earn* that place at the table?"

One little kid said something Marcus strained to hear, then he laughed. "Clarise just told me her grandpa made them sing for their supper." People laughed. "Shame on you, Mr. Willis." Marcus laughed too.

"But when we have guests, they don't have to *earn* a place at the table. We *give* it to them, right?

We share what we have with the people we love, right?" The kids nodded and said, "Yeah."

"Like Jesus gives us all a place at the table. He invites us all. And there's nothing we do to *earn* it. We have it because He loves us. He wants us to be with Him. All we have to do is accept the invitation. Will you say a prayer with me?"

She heard the simple prayer and the kids saying it back to him, but she wasn't hearing the words. Instead, she was thinking he meant this just for her and her tendency toward people pleasing—how angry she'd been at crashing their party and how worried over being accepted and not being in the way.

She didn't know what to think about it. But a hot lump she could not swallow down formed between her heart and her throat. *We share what we have with the people we love . . . accept the invitation.*

Lawrence was on stage next, reading Scripture about the birth of Christ she'd heard a thousand times or more. The words were comforting at first, but their familiarity also meant they were easy to ignore.

She went through a mental list of everything she'd packed, making sure she hadn't left anything behind. Then she made another mental list of everything she needed to buy at the grocery store once she deposited the check from the sale of her Mercedes.

The woman next to her suddenly sat up straighter, pulling Alyson out of her planning. She noticed everyone seemed to sit up straighter, as though the whole place was waking up after a short nap.

Alyson looked to the stage. Marcus's dad shook his son's hand as Lawrence went to sit back down.

Reverend Charles didn't so much speak to the crowd as set their hearts on fire. His masterful voice was his gift, and he used it like an instrument, making people lean in at times, booming his message at times, pausing dramatically at times. Energetic and vehement, he transfixed his audience. What must it have been like growing up with such a man?

She felt like clapping when he finished. An older woman two seats down, hands raised to the rafters said, "Praise Jesus, Praise Jesus! Amen, Amen, *Amen*, Brother Charles."

That was new.

People weren't clapping, but they were amening left and right.

The blue-and-silver-robed choir sang again, this time without Marcus, and people swayed in their seats. It was all very enjoyable, but it still didn't feel like church to her, it felt like an awesome multimedia seminar. She enjoyed the message but missed the ritual and comfort of the expected, the cadence and words of worship her body had experienced since childhood.

Marcus came back on stage. His father gave him a quick hug, slapping his shoulder, then sat on the far side, leaving Marcus standing in the middle. He wore a headset microphone, the cordless kind they wore on Broadway.

Looking nervous for the first time, Marcus crossed to the piano on stage. She would be, too, if she were playing in front of everyone she knew, some she hadn't seen in years. She felt for him and sent him all the encouragement she could straight from her heart. A little prayer under her breath. *You can do this, Marcus.*

He cleared his throat a little too loudly for the microphone. He smiled nervously at the audience, scanning. Alyson wondered who he was scanning for, but as soon as their gazes met, he smiled broadly, stood taller.

Her body flooded with warmth.

Seeing many faces turn her way, she smiled politely, then looked down at her hands in her lap, hoping no eyes would be on her when she glanced back up.

For once, she was thankful for being alone, not having to keep up with her children or chat with anyone. As strongly as she responded to him, she knew they could not continue being friends—it would be an ongoing torment to be so near what she could never have.

"As some of you know, it is my dream to make music for the movies out in Hollywood. In San Antonio, I've been working with the theater, writing and arranging songs for local productions.

"Forgive me if this hymn sounds a little too Broadway, but it's intended to be musical theater. It is a duet, but as I wrote it last night, I haven't had time to coach anyone else on how to sing it. Forgive the chaos. I'll do my best at both parts though they are meant to overlap at the crescendo." He sat at the piano. "Conversation with God."

He glanced at her once more, looking doubtful or worried.

"Conversation with God" was the song he wrote for *her*?

Marcus sat at the piano, thankful that he didn't have to look directly at the congregation any longer. He'd never played an original song for them before. He took a deep breath. If he took this too far, pushed too hard, it might backfire and turn her away from the church—because of something he did.

She might never forgive him.

He might never forgive himself.

He let out the breath and began with just two keys.

Two high notes. Haunting. He played slowly over and over, the second higher than the first until the chilling effect of them took hold in her bones. She recognized them. They were the two notes from the minor keys she had pressed after Darius had played for her in Marcus's piano room. These were her notes—melancholy. High and hollow.

Then he sang the words, "Dear God" in a high voice matching the notes, taking up the rest between them, so the prayer became incessant and, getting louder, despairing.

Dear God.

Why am I so lonely?

Dear God.

Why does no one care?

Dear God.

Why can't I be perfect?

Dear God.

Are you even there?

The words, the music, the tone of his voice, spread a desperate silence throughout the congregation. The notes increased in tempo, louder, more incessant, the mind given over to obsessive thoughts.

Then:

My child.

Marcus's deep voice boomed, the harmony on the piano with the left hand now, complex and bold.

I am always with you.

I'm in every smile that you meet.

Dear God.

Why can't I be perfect?

I want to be perfect.

Why can't I be perfect?

I try—

My child.

I created you as you are.

Created you for a purpose.

You must be perfectly yourself.

If you live from your heart,

You cannot live a lie—

Dear God.

Why am I lonely?

I'm afraid they won't love me.

I'm afraid to even let

them try—

My child.

Open your eyes, child.

I am here with you.

Can't you feel me hold your hand?
Dear God.
Why does everyone leave me?
Why try
when everyone will go away?
Why try
when time can take everyone away?
　　My child
Marcus's voice boomed throughout the hall.
　　If you do nothing else, love me!
　　You can't hold love and fear in the
same hand.
　　Love me!
　　I'm here with you, helping you to
stand.
　　Love me!
　　Share the love I have for you.
　　Accept the love I give to you.
　　Make the most of the love that you
have.
　　Make the most of the love that you
have.

The high minor and low major notes merged in the middle, Marcus now using the entire range of piano keys. The music beautiful and strong, and his voice deep and gentle.

　　Love one another as I love you.
　　Open yourself to me.

I exist in all creation.
Love me as I love you.
There's no reason to be lonely.
There's no reason to be perfect.
I'm here for you.
Open yourself to me.
Take my hand.

Wet drops fell on her hands clasped tightly before her heart. She wiped the tears away quickly, hoping no one saw. This was for *her*. He was trying to tell her how he felt. That he loved her. That he knew she loved him. He had said he could only express himself through music. If this song was really for her, if this was what he wanted to say, it changed *everything*.

Chapter Nineteen

The last notes hung in the air. The congregation burst forth with applause, whistles and hollers, but Alyson couldn't move.

Instead of walking off stage, left or right, Marcus took off the headset and came forward into the congregation using the steps where the children had sat. She met his gaze over the flood of people standing and rushing to him. Alyson could tell he was trying to get to her, but he was stopped by everyone wanting to speak to him, congratulate him.

She overheard people talking to him about his song, saying how it affected them, how it spoke directly to them. Their hearts, their experiences. One woman related it to her son's rehab. It was for Alyson, yet it was for everyone.

She watched his dad look on with pride as Marcus greeted people after the song. Charles finally made it to Marcus and shook his hand.

One of the members asked, "Does this mean you're staying, Marcus?"

His dad answered for him, "No. Marcus isn't meant to preach to the choir. He's taking God's message to the masses. Out there where they need it most." His dad's eyes glistened. "I'm going to miss you, Marcus. I get it now." His dad gave him a big back- slapping hug. "I had no idea you'd gotten so good."

Alyson watched the tearful hug and was so happy he had smoothed things over with his father. She'd never known what the trouble was between them but knew Marcus felt he couldn't please him, just like she couldn't please her mother.

His dad now beamed with pride.

She met Marcus's gaze again, and he seemed to apologize with his eyes. There were too many people, and everyone wanted to talk to him. But the intensity of his look and the nod of his head meant he would find her when he could. She nodded her understanding as if he had said it aloud.

There was a big potluck in the meeting hall after the service, and she followed people into the room, avoiding his family, anyone she would have to talk to.

She was thankful Andre was in the nursery and Darius still hung out with the gaggle of boys his age, saying goodbye like she'd told him to. Like she was supposed to be doing—like she had planned before she had heard his song.

She was still stunned she'd felt so much. Even now, her breathing deepened and quickened as if ready for tears. She calmed herself and stepped outside into the chilly late-December afternoon.

Children ran past. She wanted to be alone, so she walked farther out toward a picnic table under a colorful tree still losing its leaves. Here behind the church, she couldn't hear the highway. It was a safe space with a large vegetable garden and fruit trees in a row. A fence of rose bushes. A place she could think.

Did he love her? More importantly, was he *in love* with her? Was she in love with him? If she could love anyone, it was him. So kind and generous and funny and playful. Exactly what she needed to balance her.

A new pain ripped at her heart as she realized she needed to talk to her mom, wished she could talk to her dad. He would know what she really felt. He'd know how to draw it out of her. Her mom's voice sounded in her head: *Don't fall for someone just because he's nice to you. Don't make the same mistake twice.*

She couldn't help but replay in her mind the heartfelt "love me" in his voice and the expression on his face like he was near tears with wanting. *Love me!* She did! She did. She was more certain with every step. All she'd had to know was that it was safe to open her heart.

He couldn't have been more clear.

She sat at the picnic table and waited, knowing he would find her.

It wasn't long before she could hear him walking towards her through the winter-dry grass.

"I figured I'd find you outside."

"You wrote that song for me?"

"Began that way. You try to make a song universal."

"Which part is mine?"

"All of it." He sat next to her, both of them facing out.

"Did you mean it?"

"Every word." He shifted toward her. "I was afraid I was pushing too hard. That I would push you away."

She turned toward him and took his hands in hers. "It touched me. It helped me realize some things. About how I feel."

Marcus didn't say anything but seemed to expect her to continue. After a moment of awkward silence, she gathered up all her courage, leaned into him, and kissed him.

And he didn't kiss her back.

She pulled away and stared into his eyes in horror. *No. She'd been so certain.*

Marcus's face reflected the pain she felt. "I don't think you want me." His voice was gentle, almost too quiet. "I think you want God, and I'm in the way."

"What?" She looked at him a moment more, truly not understanding. Then the words clicked into place. Her face grew hot and tears began to pool, clouding her vision. "Oh, God." She covered her face. "I'm so stupid."

He reached out to comfort her, a hand on her shoulder. "No, Alyson, I—"

But she stood and walked a few steps away.

"Such a silly, stupid girl. I can't believe I'm so stupid!" She turned to him. "I thought . . . but all this time you were just being nice. You were just being wonderful you, and I took it all the wrong way. Again and again."

"Alyson. Let me explain." He shook his head as if clearing it, pain etched on his face.

"It's okay. I get it. I totally get it. The fault is all mine." She sobbed once but regained control. She would not break down in front of him—not about this. The only way to avoid total humiliation was to get away, get out of here as soon as possible and never ever see him again.

He reached for her, but she stepped back quickly, hiding her face. "We'd better get on the road, then."

"Alyson." He caught her shoulders, but she shrugged out of his grasp. "Please, let's go back to the house. Don't leave like this. Give me a chance to—"

"Don't!" She sobbed. She hid her face behind the back of her hand. "Stop being nice to me, Marcus. I don't know what to do with it."

She ran a few steps, then slowed, continuing to wipe burning tears from her face so his family wouldn't know.

ﾟ∾ﾟ

His breath left him as he watched her walk away. He'd rehearsed his little speech in his head all the way out here. Ready to help her mend her relationship with God. Ready to apologize for acting the way he had all weekend when he knew she just wanted to be friends. Ready and certain this was the way.

But when she kissed him, his carefully planned speech shattered. He *should* have reacted like any other red-blooded man and kissed her back, but honestly? He'd been so shocked that this blushing, retreating, always-trying-to-be-proper woman had the gumption to be so assertive. *Fascinating.*

Too late. He'd blown it. Shocked, he had mumbled a shard of his rehearsed speech, trying to reclaim control and do the right thing.

While writing the song last night, he'd had an epiphany—when she set those big, bright eyes so adoringly on him, she was only responding to God working through him, responding to someone being good to her for once. He shouldn't take advantage.

He caught sight of her profile as she neared the door. She paused and wiped her face. Transformed. She once again stood tall, stiff and proper. Just like she was at work.

He felt a burning, gnawing sensation in his gut as he followed her in, now realizing that she had wanted him as much as he wanted her. And he'd screwed that up beyond repair.

He hadn't made anything better. He'd just made everything worse. Much worse.

"Thank you so much for your hospitality, Mrs. Powell." Alyson stood behind Dottie where she sat eating and hugged her shoulders lightly. "I honestly haven't had such a great time in years. You made it so Darius got to have a real Christmas, and I can't thank you enough for that."

"Are you leaving already?" Dottie turned in her seat, straining to see her. "Did you get something to eat yet?" Dottie waved toward the copious casseroles on the buffet. "You can't leave till you have some food in you. Can't let you go hungry."

"Oh no, thank you. We need to get going. Really, I should've left yesterday." She felt her smile falter. *Definitely* should've left yesterday. She could've saved herself a world of embarrassment. She was so stupid to think he wanted her like she wanted him. Why on earth would he? Why would anyone?

Gail got up from her seat and hugged her. "We got one thing over you white girls—you can't hide worth a darn the fact that you've been crying. You're all splotchy, my friend."

Alyson laughed into the sobs and clung to Gail as if she were her own sister.

"Oh, now, honey, what's wrong?" Mama Dottie stood and put her arms around them both. "We loved having you. You can come back any time."

Alyson pulled away and sniffed. She was sick of crying. She hated crying in public, but she just couldn't stop. "No. I think this is it. I've messed this up pretty bad. It was so good to meet you all. Please say goodbye to the others for me."

"Alyson!" Marcus's voice barely carried over the din of the potluck festivities, everywhere people laughing and talking. But she'd heard it like a tuning fork vibrating her heart.

She met his sorrowful gaze and knew he wanted to apologize. For what? For being a gentleman? For giving them a wonderful week and a lovely holiday with family? He'd done nothing wrong. She'd thrown herself at him, and he . . .

If she could apologize for being such a pathetic mess, she would. Instead, she took advantage of the distance, of the people surrounding him, wanting to chat, wanting to congratulate him on his performance.

Without another word, she left the women. She still had just enough dignity to fetch her children and get on the road. She would leave her broken heart here. Distance was what she needed now.

Chapter Twenty

Marcus spied her at her car, putting Andre in the car seat. He jogged toward her, afraid she would have time to drive away if he walked. "Alyson! Don't leave without saying goodbye."

She closed the back door of the car and leaned against it as he approached.

"Listen, Marcus. You have real talent. And your family stands with you. So now there's nothing holding you back. You should leave for California as soon as you can."

"I'm not ready yet. I need more references, more work under my belt, something to show. Why are we even talking about this?" He'd finally figured out what he'd say if she were still upset about the kiss, and now this?

"You know what I'm hearing? A bunch of excuses." She poked his chest with her index finger. "You've got everything you need. The only reason you're stalling is because you're afraid. You're a coward."

He flinched in surprise. This was not going the way he thought it would.

She shook her head. "No. That's not true. You have the courage to create, the courage to get up on stage, and the courage to share your gift. So why don't you leave, already?" She'd poked his chest with each 'courage' and now pushed him. "Go. Put yourself out there for real. You have everything you need. What's stopping you?"

What to say? He couldn't tell her how he felt when she was slinging this mocked-up anger his way, like a coach. Believing in him more than anyone else ever had. It wasn't at all what he expected. He'd expected a chance to apologize, explain himself.

She reached into her pocket and pulled out a slip of paper and pushed it into his hand. "This is a list of contacts. I called everybody I knew in New York who could help. Most of these numbers are friends of friends of friends, so the connection is weak at best. But there's this one guy"—she pointed to the list— "he's here in Houston."

Marcus saw the shift in her demeanor. Her eyes sparkled, and her lips perked at the corners, showing her excitement. For him. She stepped closer and made sure he saw where she pointed. Jackson Dyer. Familiar name, but he couldn't place it.

"He spends half his time in New Orleans. He used to be a sports agent but now works to promote New Orleans in the film industry and promote

NOLA Jazz worldwide. I got his name from her."
She pointed to one of the New York names.

"She managed the dance studio I belonged to
and worked with him on some documentary.
Anyway, he's your best bet. She's already talked to
him about you, and he's willing to give you a listen
and point you to one of his Hollywood contacts
who can help you, but it's up to you. All I can do is
give you this list." She closed his fingers around it.

It felt so final. She believed in him more than
anyone, and she'd found a possible contact for him.
He wanted to be happy about it, but he felt numb.
"Why . . .?" He didn't know what to say.

Now that he knew she wanted him, it felt like
they were just getting started—and yet she was
trying to get rid of him.

"Marcus, you want to make sure everyone is
happy and taken care of. Don't let that sidetrack
you from your dream. Don't let anything weigh you
down or hold you back. Including us."

"Please stay one more day. I'm sorry. I say
stupid things when I'm nervous, okay? Let's figure
this out. Stay. Please."

"I can't. I have too much to do. Big decisions to
make. I have to face *my* future. And you should
face *yours*." She tapped the paper in his hand.
"Promise me you'll talk to this guy. Promise."

"I will." He put the paper in his breast pocket, then held both of her hands. "Promise me you'll keep your heart open. And don't be so hard on yourself. You are worthy. You're perfect just as you are. Promise?"

He saw the same look of adoration she'd had when he'd sung to her.

"I will." But then her smile faltered. She looked away, dropped his hands. Her ears pinked. He wished he could see her face.

"I'm sorry I *misunderstood* things earlier." She met his gaze, and he could see how her cheeks and eyes reddened—it tore his heart.

"I hope..." Her voice broke. She stared straight ahead. She exhaled heavily, her shoulders sagging as if deflated. "Never mind." She stepped back and offered her hand to shake. "Thank you for everything, Marcus. Take care of yourself."

She shook his hand like they were strangers. Like they hadn't danced in the kitchen. Like he hadn't held her in his arms.

He had no words, couldn't believe it was ending this way.

She stepped around the hood of the car, and he didn't do the gentlemanly thing and walk her to the door.

He could barely breathe—crumbled like a brick smashed by a sledgehammer.

He heard a knock on the car window and looked down.

Darius waved. "See you next year!" He yelled from inside, smiling at his own joke.

She got in the car.

A moment later they drove away.

If she looked back, he couldn't tell.

He stood out in the cold wind till he could see them no more.

Chapter Twenty-One

"Marcus? Marcus, where'd you run off to?"

He ignored his mother's voice and continued staring at the ceiling of his childhood room, lying where Alyson had slept just hours ago.

It didn't take Mama and Gail long to find him. He should have gone somewhere else.

"What's wrong, baby? Everybody missed you at fellowship. Why'd you run off? You not feeling well?"

"He's moping, Mama. He screwed things up with Alyson."

"Shut up, Gail." He sat upright on the bed, uncomfortable being prone with Gail's arrows flying.

"Is that true, Marcus? She was pretty upset when she left."

He bent forward, elbows on knees, head in his hands. He didn't want to talk about this.

His mom sat on the bed and rubbed his back like he was a child. "Baby, what happened?"

Now he was caught. He'd missed his chance to walk out. He couldn't be rude to Mama. Sighing heavily, he tried to find the words, wanting to keep it private. "She told me how she felt and I kind of . . . didn't. I froze."

"You idiot!" Gail's arrows hit their mark. "You think you can do better than her, you're crazy!"

"I didn't say that, Gail! Stop yelling at me."

"Oh, I'm not yelling yet. That's for after I hear what dumb thing you did."

He ignored Gail's scorn and looked his mom in the eye. "I thought she was about to open up about her relationship with God and then . . ."

"What, baby? What happened?"

His mom's closeness was suffocating, the soothing rub, irritating. He stood. He couldn't admit what he had done. Or rather, hadn't done. Too embarrassing.

He'd had everything he wanted within his grasp, but she left because he couldn't take action when it was called for.

Story of his life. Too impulsive or too cautious when it counted, no wisdom to help him balance the two.

She was right—he should already be in L.A. He thought he was being smart waiting when really, he was a coward.

But this time, he wasn't just beating himself up for a bad decision. This time, his entire being yelled out, "Go Back!" like he was now on a wrong path. It was a physical pain, an irritation under his skin, in his bones.

He walked out past Gail and Mama, hearing them call after him but not caring. He had to work this out of his system. He had to *do something*, even if it was something that wouldn't get her back. How could he? She'd made her choice.

Marcus pushed against the weighted bar, his arms shaking. He grunted through gritted teeth until he got the bar secured back in its cradle. He sat up, dazed by the effort of his hours-long workout. Exhausted, he glanced around the garage, becoming aware of the cold as his sweat evaporated.

He'd surely hurt in the morning. Good. That's what he wanted. He hurt now. In a few hours, he wouldn't even be able to lift his arms over his head. He wanted to sleep the rest of the time he was here, anyway.

He didn't want to talk to anyone. They'd just ask questions he couldn't answer. Like 'why?' Why did he freeze when he now knew he wanted her more than he'd ever wanted anything? And why did it take her walking away for him to realize that?

As he sat, the sweat on his bare back chilled in the cold seeping through the garage doors.

"Marcus? Supper's on."

His dad. But he was never sent to announce supper. And it couldn't be that late already, could it?

"Not hungry."

His dad came a few steps into the garage. Examined him over his glasses. "You know, the way you two look at each other, the way you've already started talking in 'we' and 'us,' you're not just friends. Whether you admit it or not."

At first, he was taken aback by the notion his father had been watching them, taken aback by the notion his father had any interest at all. "Not you, too, Dad. Did Mom put you up to this?"

"Do you love her?"

Marcus nodded. "Yeah." He shrugged. "Maybe. I don't know."

"How could you not know?" His dad's incredulous tone focused Marcus's attention. "That's the one thing in life I never once doubted. I even doubted my calling, resisted it in the early days." Dad sat on the weight-lifting bench with him.

"Really?"

"Of course! I grew up poor, so I wanted security above all else. I didn't want to devote my life to people I hardly knew. But God kept after me. And I surrendered eventually. But surrendering to your mother?" His dad broke out into a wide smile Marcus rarely saw. "That was immediate. I knew she was the woman for me the first time I met her."

Marcus bent forward, resting his elbows on his knees, his muscles shaky and weak. He'd overdone it. That's what he deserved.

His dad mirrored him. "Want to know a secret? I had to break her down little by little just like God had to break me down. Love takes a whole lot of faith, son. And faith is a great leap into the unknown." Silence. Then, in a stronger voice, "Do you love this woman?"

"Yes." Marcus breathed in a ragged breath and let it out in a huff. "But I've messed things up, Dad. She doesn't want me now. Our lives are going in different directions, anyway. She's got her future. I've got mine. That's what she said." That's what had hurt the most.

"Marcus. You live best when you live from your heart. Don't talk yourself out of love."

In his heart, Marcus felt like she was his, that their love was an irresistible and mysterious force, like an underwater current connecting oceans.

But his thoughts had become jumbled with ideas of leading her on and wanting to give her room to heal from her broken marriage and thinking maybe God *did* put him in her path just to help lead her to

Him. He questioned his own motives all along the way.

And yet, his heart knew only this: he wanted Alyson to be happy, he wanted to make her smile, he wanted to make her feel loved.

But he kept reliving the horror in her eyes the moment she realized he was not kissing her back. The way she had stammered and apologized and beat herself up for his failing. The burning humiliation in her cheeks.

He had hurt her. He didn't deserve her.

Marcus hung his head—she must hate him now. She must think he was a coward. A hypocrite. A liar.

"If you love her, go after her." Dad squeezed Marcus's shoulder, relieving the tension that had built. "Convince her. It's as simple as that. Other than deciding to do God's work in this world, there is no bigger decision than who you will choose as your wife, your partner for life."

His father pulled his shoulder back, forcing him to look him in the eye. Marcus felt like a puppet— no strength left in him to resist. "Son, if you want her, go get her. If you could see the way she looks at you."

Marcus closed his eyes and imagined her before him. That look of pure adoration was what had confused him most. That kind of look was meant for God, not him. No one had ever looked at him like that before.

And yet the closer they got, the harder she pushed him away. Why? He remembered her angry outburst in the park—unlovable, marked as an adulteress by her divorce.

Marcus sat up straighter with the realization she'd been trying to save him from the same fate— that's why she pushed him away early on. And what she'd said about not letting anything hold him back from his dreams, including her—that's why she pushed him away now. At every turn, she'd protected him.

He appreciated his dad talking to him and was still a little shocked he had. But he wanted to be alone now. He had to think.

"Thanks, Dad." Marcus took a deep breath and stood. "I'll go get cleaned up."

He grabbed his shirt and blazer from the pile of boxes he'd set them on, and a note fell out. He picked it up— the page of contacts Alyson had given him. Alyson, his biggest fan and supporter. Even after he'd broken her heart.

"Son, I know you don't want to hear it, but I'm going to warn you against spending too much time alone right now."

"No, Dad, you don't have to worry. It's not like before."

"Your mother worries about you, son."

Marcus smiled at that, considering it was his father's worried, pleading eyes before him. "I'm okay, Dad. This isn't like when Gramps died. You and Mom don't need to worry about me being alone. Honest. I'm okay."

He met his father's gaze to give him some reassurance. His dad nodded, but the heartbreaking worry in his eyes didn't lessen.

"Now I need to be alone to think. I've got some planning to do if I'm going to get her back."

Dad clapped him on the back and gave him a rough hug, still strong. "That's my boy."

Chapter Twenty-Two

Alyson double-checked she'd locked the door before turning in. It had been a long night already, the night before school started again. Reining in Darius's excitement over participating in the school play with Marcus and Mrs. Allen was no easy task.

She'd managed Darius's expectations by reminding him it wouldn't happen immediately, that Marcus—who he needed to call Mr. Powell from now on—couldn't give him the attention he'd paid him over Christmas. Mr. Powell couldn't play favorites, and Darius needed to let the other kids have his attention too.

That was her, always the naysayer, the boss, the meany. But she wanted her boys to understand that disappointment was inevitable—she didn't want it to surprise and hurt them when it came.

Marcus had a way of making bad news acceptable and even fun. Go with the flow. Have faith. But wishing for a faith as strong as Marcus's would not make it so. Tracking details, planning, budgeting, scheduling, checking and double-checking was what would give her security and certainty. Going with the flow could make them homeless.

She packed the work she'd been doing at the kitchen table into the banker's box Marcus had carried for her that fateful night their friendship began. She'd hoped they would remain friends but hadn't been able to say it out loud after her stupid little speech at the car. If she'd said it, he probably would have stopped by just to be nice and friendly, throwing her onto the rollercoaster of hope and doubt all over again. Better not to hope at all.

He hadn't come by, hadn't called. She regretted slamming that door shut so tightly, but couldn't see another way, even now.

Besides, wanting him in her life was selfish. He made her laugh, made her feel beautiful and wanted, made her feel taken care of. But she had nothing to offer, and she would not be in another uneven relationship. She'd rather do it alone. She could depend on herself. Everyone else eventually let you down. Even family.

She turned out the light over the box of paperwork and made her way down the hall toward the bedroom.

Knock knock knock. So soft, she almost missed it.

For a breathless moment, she stood totally still. Her heart leaped at the thought it was Marcus. She quick-stepped to the door in fuzzy-slippered feet and peeked through the peephole. She could just make out that he was blowing on his hands. What was he doing out without a jacket?

She opened the door just as he was getting ready to knock again, his hand hovering. "Marcus, what are you doing here?"

"Hey." His worried brow relaxed with his smile. "Sorry it's so late. I just wanted to make sure you're okay. You didn't answer my texts."

"I didn't get any texts."

He raised his brows. "Uh-oh. Some stranger knows way too much about me now, then." He chuckled. "He's probably hiding by his door with a baseball bat, waiting for some strange guy to show up. Oops."

A cold wind blew, and he hunched his shoulders against it.

"Goodness, it's cold. Come in, come in."

He shuffled inside, and she closed the door behind him.

"Thanks. I didn't count on the wind chill."

"The boys are asleep," she said softly.

"Sorry," he whispered.

They stood awkwardly for a moment. She was suddenly aware of her dumpy flannel pajamas and silly lamb slippers her sister had sent her for Christmas. She crossed her arms, uncomfortable standing before him without a bra.

"How's the car?" His eyes looked sad. He wasn't really asking about the car.

She sat on the settee near the door. As he sat next to her his melancholy turned a shade more grim, like this already wasn't going the way he'd thought it would. What had he been hoping for?

"The car's great. I mean, it's no Mercedes, but it drives well. I like it. It'll be good for us."

"Good. Good. That's great news."

Another awkward silence as he sat studying his hands. She'd been the one totally humiliated, so why was he the nervous one? "Did you call the number I gave you?"

He brightened. "Yeah. Cool cat. We've talked a couple of times, even met over drinks. You were right. He's setting me up. I've got a lot more contacts now through him. I owe you one."

"It's all about who you know."

"Yeah, he said the same."

Back to the anxious silence and fidgeting hands.

"Cute little lambs." Marcus nodded at her slippers.

"Thanks." She held her feet out straight and bounced the lambs, their little ears flopping back and forth. "A gift from my sister."

"How is your mom adjusting to . . . where is she again?"

Definitely stalling. Why? "She's happier than she's been in a long time. You know, everything here just reminded her she didn't have Daddy anymore. Everything is new out there, and she's got my sister's newborn to gush over. She's just waiting for the money the sale of this house will bring."

"And then what?" His gaze burned into hers with an intensity that stopped her thoughts. It took her a moment to recover.

"Um. I've narrowed down a few apartment complexes. Two of them would put Darius in a different school come fall, but Mom is going to give me some money from the sale. That will help us start over. Maybe, if all the money timing works out, we can stay in the neighborhood." She didn't want to talk about her money troubles. She'd never get to sleep if they focused on it much longer.

"Marcus, what's—"

"Alyson, when—"

"You go ahead," he said. "Ladies first."

"I was just going to ask you why you were here. You didn't really come all this way in the cold just to ask about the car."

"I . . ." He faced her. "When you kissed me, did you mean it?"

Instant anger rose, bubbling from deep inside. "Did I mean it? What kind of question is that?"

"Shh, the boys."

"Don't you shush me!" she whispered, shooting daggers from her eyes.

He put up his hands in surrender.

"Did I mean it? Why no, Marcus, I always go around throwing myself at random men." She got in his face but kept her angry voice at a whisper. "I think nothing of it. I just casually sprinkle myself around. That's so me." She crossed her arms once more.

"Come on, now. I didn't mean it like that."

"It's late, Marcus, and you and Darius have school bright and early in the morning."

"I just meant, was it because you really felt that way about *me* or were you carried away by the song?"

"You are the most infuriating man." She pressed her palms to her forehead in disbelief, then remembered why she'd kept her arms crossed and did so again. "What do you want me to say? Is this all about your ego? You want me to say you're so good that the song made me lose my mind?"

"Why are you so mad? I just want to know if it was real or just a fluke of the moment." He held her gaze, then swallowed thickly and studied his hands once more. "So you *do* regret it. I thought so."

The pain in his voice was like cold water down her spine. She hated to see him hurt. "Marcus. It wasn't a fluke. I would do it again." She leaned forward and kissed him lightly on the mouth. She had planned to say afterward, 'But it doesn't change anything.' But she hadn't counted on him kissing her back.

The passion of his kiss swept her away, washing her in warmth. He cradled her head in his hands, and she melted against his chest. She could not get close enough to him. She found herself powerless to stop. His strong arms pulled her close. His warm lips trailed down her neck, and she went limp with desire.

She knew they should stop, that this could go nowhere, but it had been so long since she'd been touched like a woman. She never wanted it to end. "Marcus." Her tone was too breathy even to her own ears. They had to stop while she still had will enough to do so. She had to get control before she fell into the deep end.

He brought his hand to her hair and pulled away as if he could read her thoughts, as if he, too, was trying to regain control.

"Marcus." She'd finally found her voice, both her hands against his chest but not pushing him away. She wanted him—this—so badly. But they had to be strong.

"We need to stop. I know." He rested his forehead against hers, holding her still. They remained like that until their breathing calmed, their sensibility returned.

When he released her, she missed his warm embrace. How intimate it was to be so close even though their passion had ceased. She'd love to be in his arms like this forever. Just being. Together.

He sighed deeply. "I missed you."

"I missed you too. But, Marcus, we barely know each other. It was only a long weekend."

"I know you well enough to miss you. I've missed you every day since you left. I had no one to play with."

"Were we playing? Is that why you came here tonight? To play?"

"Come on, Alyson. Don't do me that way. You know I'm not like that."

She sighed. He was right. He was always right. But it didn't change the fact that she didn't have *time* to play. She had to stay focused. It wasn't that she was mad at Marcus. She was mad at herself. Knowing how much she wanted him didn't change anything, it just made it harder to do the right thing. Neither of them had time to play.

"You should probably go, Marcus. It's late, and I know you have to be at work at 6:30."

"I want to see you again." He pressed his palms together as if in prayer. "I promise I'll behave."

She met his gaze. He still burned. Every breath she took did nothing to strengthen her resolve. The longer she looked in his eyes the more danger there was in being consumed in that fire. She didn't trust *herself* to behave.

She looked away. "I'm working ten days straight."

"I'll bring you dinner. You like Thai food?"

"Marcus. I like you. A lot. But this isn't going to work. My number one priority is providing for my boys. Number two is spending every waking moment with them when I'm not working."

"Are you saying you *don't* want to see me again?"

She looked down. She couldn't say it, couldn't lie.

He shifted in his seat like it had thorns. "I want to hear you say it. Out loud. Loud and clear."

"You'll be on your way to Hollywood this summer, right?" She tried meeting his gaze again but couldn't face him. "We might be leaving this neighborhood at any time between now and then, anyway. It's all so up in the air and temporary. I can't do temporary, Marcus. I'm not built that way. I need something lasting to hold onto."

She stood and walked to the door. "I'm sorry. I wish we'd met at a different time. A more settled time. Long distance doesn't work, and I won't be the reason you miss your chance in Hollywood. I believe in you too much to hold you back." She opened the door, a cold wind blowing in.

He stood, looking like he was trying to make up his mind what to say, but his lips just clenched down tighter. "Goodnight." He walked out without looking her way.

She closed the door and leaned against it, the cold seeping into her flannel top.

She'd done the right thing releasing them both. So why did it feel like she'd ruined any chance at happiness? Why did it feel like she'd smashed her own heart in that closed door?

She longed to be in his arms again. Some kind of magic, the calm she felt in his arms, surrounded by love.

And she'd put an end to that. For good reasons.

Why was doing the right thing so hard?

She saw many lonely years stretch before her.

She'd never meet another man like Marcus.

Chapter Twenty-Three

The next Sunday, as Marcus sat cramped in the tiny A/V booth of Redeemer Lutheran getting the slide deck ready for services, he heard a man call out "Alyson, over here."

It couldn't be.

But his head popped up, and he zeroed in on the sound before he'd thought twice about it. And there she was, shaking Hector's hand. She tried to shake his wife Maria's hand but got pulled into a hug. How did Alyson know Hector? Did she know Marcus was here?

He watched as the boys met Hector's middle-schoolers and sat with them. Alyson walked up to the altar and kneeled before the large, wooden cross. She crossed herself, paused a long moment, then crossed herself again before rising.

Marcus had only seen that before in movies.

She turned and walked back to her pew, looking around at the walls and stained-glass windows with interest, as if she were looking for something in particular.

He ducked slightly but knew she wouldn't see him in the booth. He was as good as camouflaged.

As she continued to gaze up at the stained glass, he couldn't take his eyes off the way she glowed.

Even as he hid, his heart swelled. She was here. She was here in God's house, not because Marcus had invited her, not because she'd promised to hear him sing, but because she *wanted* to be.

Like she'd said, no one was going to change her. She'd come in and practiced her own rituals, honoring God—and maybe her father's memory— her own way. But she'd taken what he'd sung to her to heart and allowed God into her life again.

He was so proud of her his heart would burst. His eyes prickled with unformed tears. It was all worth it. He could accept the heartache, the loneliness, knowing that maybe he had something to do with her turning to face God again. He wanted to holler to the rafters!

The organ sounded as the pastor walked down the center aisle to the pulpit. Marcus readied the slide deck for the announcements. Then he sat back and closed his eyes. "Thank you, Lord, for letting me see this," he whispered. Just when he had begun to doubt his new plan, God had sent him a sign. Which was good because his new plan was a real leap of faith.

༄

Alyson was so confused. She had thanked God for giving her the strength to say no to Marcus, and yet, now God had put him in her path again.

Here she sat with him in one of the big corner booths in their favorite diner. Her boys sat between them, Hector's family sat on her left side. An old widower neighbor Hector looked after sat in a regular chair in the gap of the circle, across from her, his walker next to him.

Alyson was going to have a few angry words with the Almighty when she had a moment to herself. Until then, she'd have to sit in this mild embarrassment, not knowing what to say to Marcus.

Every time she looked at him, she felt his lips on hers, felt the heat of his embrace. And still, although her mind now knew otherwise, her heart still felt the rejection of two weeks ago.

"Hey, if you keep feeding Andre, your breakfast will get cold," Marcus said.

Darius looked at her and then at her plate as if this was a surprise—like he'd never noticed she didn't eat when they did, but after.

Of course, as soon as Darius had seen Marcus at the church, he'd latched on to him and had forgotten all about her and his little brother. This was the first time he'd stopped talking since he'd seen Marcus. Whatever Marcus said was golden to her little boy.

"I can warm it up at work."

"Marcus," Hector said, still chewing, "I just pieced it together. You were the Singing Elf, weren't you? At Della."

"Yep. That was me."

She noticed he said it without the irritation he'd surrounded it with before. Now it was just a fact.

"Did *not* even recognize you. Never saw past the elf costume." Hector looked at his watch, the face glowing with an alarm. He touched the side, not bothering to put down his fork. "Almost time to go, kids, finish up."

Alyson glanced at her watch. Yes, they had little time left before work. She sighed. It would be the boys' first day at a new twenty-four-hour anytime-drop-off daycare. With strangers. She hated this.

"Y'all both opening today?" Marcus asked.

"Yes," she said, and Hector nodded, shoveling the last of his breakfast into his mouth. He signaled the waitress—a newbie Alyson didn't know—for more coffee, by holding up the empty cup. Maybe not smooth, but effective. She came at once.

"You should sing with the choir, Marcus," Hector said.

The old man across from them, who had said little during the breakfast, cackled. "Those old ladies need a good deep voice to balance out their warbling. Heh heh."

Everyone laughed, but Hector's teen boys laughed the loudest and jostled each other with elbows. Seemed to be a point of contention for them, the high-pitched, screechy hymns.

"Was great to break the fast with y'all, but it's time to *vamanos*." Hector drained his coffee. His wife was already out of the booth and unfolding the old man's walker.

"Thanks for inviting us," Alyson said.

"The invitation is always open." Maria smiled, then pushed her gangly teen boy forward, his face in his phone. She waited for Mr. Joe, the old man, to walk before her. "Great to meet you finally, Alyson. See you next Sunday?"

Alyson nodded, not wanting to speak a promise she might not be able to keep, even though she'd felt welcome there. She was on a hunt to find a new church family. There had to be a place where she fit.

"See you soon." Hector pointed at her. Then he shook Marcus's hand. "You should join us for the Thursday night men's Bible study, Marcus. Bunch of ornery cuss's like Mr. Joe here make it funny. Man, they pull no punches. It's hilarious."

"Sounds good. I'll try to make it."

Hector nodded, picked up the ticket for their food, then waved at Darius and Andre.

And so they were alone. Together.

They were silent a moment, staring at each other, unable to say what needed to be said, if they even knew what that was. Darius looked from her to Marcus and back. "Can I have money for the claw?"

Alyson grinned. She gave him a dollar and told him to mind Luisa, who was operating the register this busy morning.

Darius wasn't more than a few steps away before Marcus said, "I miss you."

He latched two of his fingers around two of hers, as if that small touch was all they could bear. Luckily, her very needy toddler chose that moment to ram his head into her shoulder, breaking their contact, so she didn't have to.

Andre rubbed his eyes though he'd only been awake for four hours—he was always sleepy after a meal—and clung to her. She clung to him, like a life jacket keeping her afloat, keeping her head above her heart.

"You're leaving for California in June. Is that right?" She tried to sound casual as she held Andre with her right hand and tried to eat with her left. It was slow going. Best weight-loss diet ever.

Marcus scooted close and took her fork from her, loaded it with eggs and fed her. The deliberate motions held an intensity she couldn't take. Not now that she knew any possibility of them being a couple was over. He was leaving. The end of them was happening, but in slow motion. Just to rip her heart out.

"Yeah. Dad's warning about music education getting de-funded came to pass. They decided to fire half of the elementary music teachers and make the ones they keep cover two schools." He cut another bite for her. Too big. Man-sized.

"They cut the funding but didn't cut the program?" This time she took the fork rather than let him feed her. It was romantic, but she didn't want romance. Plus, any stains on her white blouse would require a wardrobe change prior to work, and that wasn't factored into her timetable.

"Yeah, they chopped it, but didn't eliminate it. My principal asked me to stay, but I couldn't allow them to RIF or fire someone else when this is just a stepping stone for me. And Jackie—she's at Enchanted Oaks elementary—she's got two kids in high school and is close to twenty years in the same district. It means more to her to stay and keep her job."

He sat back and stretched his arm across the back of the booth. "They're ruining it, though. How can you build a rapport with the kids if you only see them twice a month? That's no way to teach music."

Andre took Marcus's open arms as an invitation and stumbled across the booth to him, thumb in mouth. He used Marcus's bicep to hide behind while he peered over at the people in the next booth, an older woman playing peek-a-boo with him.

Alyson smiled warmly at her, then took the opportunity to eat her already cold breakfast.

"Means a lot of burned out, traveling teachers in the district, but since music and the arts aren't on the state exam, the powers that be don't care about them."

"And you're not mad? Is anyone fighting this?"

"Of course I'm mad—the human brain develops with music and art well before the introduction of math and reading. A healthy brain needs music and art to develop to its highest potential. These lawmakers are shortsighted at best. Ruining a whole generation at worst. But at least they didn't outright kill the program. No one wanted that on their record when re-election comes around."

She loved this new fire in his eyes and tone. They'd stayed away from controversial topics during the holiday weekend—Dottie pushing anyone who wanted to discuss politics outside as if they were as noxious as smokers. Alyson wanted to know more about what drove him, what fired him up inside.

But the time for that had passed.

They needed to rip off this Band-Aid because seeing each other hurt. The fact he wasn't pressuring her to see him again meant he too must realize how hopeless it was. "So why not leave now?"

He looked at her like she was nuts. "I have a contract. And the kids. I'm not leaving them mid-year. We've got a show to put on, you know." He smiled.

"Yes, I know. It's all Darius talks about. *Percussionist*. Thanks for that." She crossed her eyes and stuck out her tongue to show the constant 'practicing' was driving her batty, though she knew Darius loved it.

He laughed, and they shared silence for a moment, their amusement quickly dissolving into tension again. He twirled an unused straw in his fingers and tapped out a tune on the table. All the while, his sad eyes cast downward.

"Darius doesn't know I'm leaving yet. I'm not telling the kids until the end of the school year. Then they'll have a whole summer to forget about me."

"Impossible." She tried to smile but sitting here talking so casually about him leaving was breaking her heart. And she could tell by the way he softened as he looked at her that he felt it too.

"Alyson—"

His gentle tone made her ache. He was going to ask to see her again, and she didn't know if she could be strong enough this time. But it was hopeless. They were living different lives, going in different directions.

She forced her gaze to her watch rather than be caught in those amber eyes. "Oh, boy. I better round up Darius. We've got to go, or I'm going to be late." She hurriedly collected Andre's things into the diaper bag.

"Hey. How did you find out I was leaving in June?"

"Gail called and invited me to the Fourth of July party at your parents' place. Even though you won't be there."

"Gail." He shook his head and sighed. "What else did she tell you?"

"Nothing about you. Don't go getting your ego in a wad."

He laughed at the mixed metaphor.

"Believe it or not, she just wanted another divorcée to talk to. She's thinking about dating again. Big step."

They had talked, and cried, for hours together just a couple days ago. Gail had asked, "How do you know when you're ready?" Alyson had replied, "I think when the anger is gone, you can love again. Before that, it's a waste of time to even try."

And in talking with Gail and trying to get her to a place where she could forgive her ex, Alyson realized she had already forgiven hers. She had accepted her reality. Preferred it.

Mama Dottie's plea for her to remember that she had been set free . . . Marcus opening her eyes to new interpretations of troublesome Scriptures . . . Oddly enough, changing the way she saw her situation changed everything about it. Once she saw it as God setting her free from a bad marriage, forgiving Will became much easier.

Darius appeared by her side clutching a neon green whale with googly eyes. Where did they get these off-brand plush toys? "I won! I won! Lookit!"

Andre turned at the sound of excitement and reached for the plush toy, stepping on Marcus, who grabbed him around the middle before he took a nose-dive to the floor below.

Darius gave it to him, much her relief. The whale went straight into Andre's mouth.

"Mom, you owe Luisa another dollar."

"Okay, okay. Get your things, please, we need to get going."

Marcus picked up their meal tickets while she struggled with Andre and the diaper bag.

"You don't have to do that." She grunted as Andre jumped into her arms again rather than walk.

"Least I could do. Besides, you've got your arms full. You go on, so you're not late."

"Oh. Okay. Thank you." She hesitated, standing before him, waiting for ... what? Darius walked down the aisle toward the door. "Um. Goodbye, then."

"Nope. No time for goodbyes." He escorted her and Andre to the front of the noisy diner, his hand once again at her lower back, a hum of electricity up her spine.

She didn't want to leave like this. There was more to be said. Wasn't there? But there wasn't time.

He broke from them and went to the register, turning back to wave.

She left, feeling somehow dismissed.

No time for goodbyes?

She supposed they would have nothing *but* goodbyes from now until June.

Chapter Twenty-Four

Over the next few weeks, breakfast after the early service turned into Sunday night dinners at Alyson's.

It started one Sunday when the daycare was suddenly closed—no warning, just locked and dark—and Alyson had called him in a panic asking if he knew anyone who could watch her boys. Maybe one of the teens from the church? Could he ask?

"Just bring them back to the church. I'm here till three every Sunday. They can stay in the daycare for as long as I'm here."

"Thank you thank you thank you! A million thank yous. I'll see if I can get off work early. I would call in, but I'm the only manager today."

"Just give Darius your key, and I'll take the boys home and wait for you there."

Silence. "You'd do that?"

"Of course. Gotta go. Second service is starting. Tell the daycare attendant I'm picking up the boys. She knows me. Piece of cake. Bye now."

He'd hung up nearly jumping in his seat. He pointed to the rafters. *Smooth move, Father God, smooth move.*

And each Sunday since then, they'd followed the same plan.

Last Sunday, he and the boys went shopping and got dinner started by the time Alyson came home. Marcus had taken a chance—many women wouldn't want someone messing up their kitchen—but when she had gotten home and took in the sight of him cooking while the boys worked in activity books, she'd given him the biggest bear hug.

He wanted another one of those hugs, real bad. He'd searched online all week for a recipe that was foolproof.

Marcus glanced at the clock on the stove as he put the chicken and rice dish in the oven. "Hey, Darius, isn't your mom usually home by now?"

Darius looked up, oblivious.

Keys jangled, and the lock turned. He went to greet her, but this time he knew by the shocked and sorrowful look on her face as she opened the door that there would be no bear hug. She still held her phone in her hand. Bad news.

"What's wrong?"

She dropped her bag on the settee. Set her phone beside it. Removed her jacket as if the movement pained her.

"It's happening." She looked up at him, her pretty lips turned down. "I thought we'd have more time."

"What? What's wrong?"

"We've got two people trying to outbid each other with earnest money for the house. The real estate agent was so excited, I couldn't get a word in edgewise." She leaned into him then, with her arms crossed over her heart.

He pulled her close, and she melted against him.

"Every time I start to feel comfortable, it's like another rug gets pulled out from under me."

Darius came around the corner, Andre on his heels.

She stepped away and put on a smile for them. "So what did you two do today?"

"Do we have to move again? Like last time?" Darius's whole body tensed like he was ready to bolt down the hallway.

"No, honey, not like last time." Alyson sat on the edge of the settee and held out her arms for her boy. He ran into them. Andre followed. "It might be another month or two before we go. It won't be scary. This time, it will be planned. Well thought out. Not like last time."

"I don't want to change schools, Mom. I'm a percussionist." His words muffled against her shoulder.

"I know, sweetie. I'll do everything I can."

"Don't even worry about it. Not for a second." Marcus didn't think he'd said anything wrong until Alyson gave him an exasperated glare. He pushed on anyway. "There are things just around the corner you can't even dream up. The future can be a pretty exciting place."

Darius still held on to his mom but turned his head and smiled at Marcus.

Bingo.

So far, despite the bad news, this Sunday night had been a repeat of last Sunday. He'd gotten that bear hug he'd been angling for by making dinner. Alyson had washed dishes while he'd helped Darius with his math worksheets. And when it was time for her to put Andre to bed, she didn't hint that it was late. Last week they had stayed up talking until ten. He hoped for a repeat.

As he waited for her in the family room, with the TV on low, tuned to something he wasn't even watching, he rehearsed his new plan in his head. It seemed the timetable had moved up drastically.

They weren't ready.

"What's on your mind, deep thinker?" She approached, hiding a yawn behind her hand and waved his feet off the couch so she could sit.

"Nothing you need to worry about."

"Speaking of worry, please don't get Darius's hopes up too much. I have to manage his expectations. The future is not all rainbows and cotton candy."

"I meant what I said. You don't know what the future holds so there's no point in fretting over it. Plan for what you can control, otherwise give it to God."

"I know, I know. Easier for some than others. And I'm still very much in the 'others' category." She tucked her legs beneath her and faced him. "I think I can use this to my advantage. The bidding war, I mean."

"Yeah?"

"Yeah. Instead of selling the house to the highest bidder, I'll choose the one who agrees to let us stay the longest."

"Great thinking."

She yawned again. "Sorry."

"I should go." He stood.

"No, I'm not sleepy," she pleaded. "I've got to stay up to fill out shoplifter forms anyway. We had gobs of shoplifters this weekend. Maybe I should make some coffee. Want some?"

"No. And you should get some sleep and work on the forms tomorrow." He slipped his shoes back on. "Why are there more shoplifters all of a sudden?"

"Valentine's, silly. Those cute little cut-glass heart pendant and earring sets are flying off the shelves."

Valentine's Day. His stomach turned to lead. He'd forgotten about Valentine's Day. "At least it's cheap stuff, right?" He hoped he covered well.

"By design. Mr. Giles is no fool. That's why they're out in the open, away from the more expensive jewelry. But teenagers especially are stealing in time for Valentine's Day. Most desperate holiday of the year." Another yawn.

He hadn't calculated the most romantic of days into his plan. Maybe . . . but, no. Too soon. They weren't ready. She'd reject him, and then where would they be?

"Just a few days to go, then they'll start stealing bathing suits for Spring Break, and I won't have to fill out the forms anymore." Another stifled yawn. "I can't wait until Mr. Giles hires more managers. Being down two is really getting old."

He offered his hand. She took it, and he pulled her from the couch. They held hands as she walked him to the door.

He crossed the threshold, kissed her hand and said goodnight. His mind spun around possible futures, most of them turning out horribly. Only one path—the scariest—possibly turning out right. Well, maybe a fifty-fifty chance of turning out right. His gut would not stop churning over the new timetable.

On the way home, he felt a buzz in his pocket and pulled out his phone. A text from Alyson: *I miss you already.*

The one night he'd forgotten to say it! He always said it as soon as he crossed the threshold of her home. She usually rolled her eyes, but he kept doing it because her smile brought out her dimples.

He'd been so distracted he'd forgotten.

And then another text: an emoji with its tongue sticking out.

And another: a blushing kiss emoji.

Then a message: "Goodnight." Emoji with sleepy zzz's.

He looked through all of the possible emojis he could send. Finally, he merely sent the same blushing kiss emoji back to her. Such a little thing. But so huge in his heart.

Maybe Valentine's wouldn't mess up his timeline. Maybe it was time for a leap of faith.

Chapter Twenty-Five

Alyson gave the irate customer her friendliest smile, then swiped her ID on the register and poked the right sequence of buttons to start the dreaded return process. Barbara shifted from foot to foot beside her.

"Thank you, Alyson. I hate to trouble you when you're so busy. I'd do it myself if they allowed it, but, you know, just a part-timer."

Alyson reassured Barbara with a pat on her shoulder. "No worries. I'm so glad you decided to stay. We should grab lunch together sometime."

Alyson caught the older woman's emotional smile out of the corner of her eye as she quickly performed the transaction. She couldn't believe she had resisted being friends with Barb just because she was temporary. When she'd heard Barb was staying on, she'd thanked God for giving her another friend.

Thanks to Marcus, she was willing to risk a little vulnerability now. A little. Baby steps.

She looked up from the register, about to ask the customer for her card to refund her money, only to see the woman was looking beyond Alyson, open-mouthed, head tilted in curiosity.

A weird guitar chord strummed behind her, and she turned to see Marcus with his grandfather's lyre, another man with a guitar, and one with a violin. They started playing a song she didn't recognize. The guitar grounded the song in the blues while the violin soared with an Irish melody. The lyre seemed to be a good luck charm Marcus held tenderly.

"Alyson, I've realized that I can only change your mind, your heart, through song. I messed it up the first time. But this one is just us. Only us. The Song of Alyson and Marcus. Here it goes."

She saw him glance away from her and followed his gaze to see her boss giving him two thumbs up. So Mr. Giles was in on this? By the cheesy grin, she knew the answer was yes. And they were once again drawing a crowd of shoppers.

The guitarist kept the beat while Marcus played a slow melody—one that didn't match the frenetic soaring of the violin. One would play then the other, as if they were answering each other, swirling around each other, dancing with each other. Marcus's gaze burned into hers as he played. She melted as he slowly closed his eyes and began to sing:

I don't understand
Why you ask me all the time
Why it is that I want you

I don't understand
How you've reached inside my mind
And made me feel that I need you
Alyson,
you're the only one, the only one
who's ever seen me
Alyson,
You're the only one, the only one
Who helps me be me
Alyson,
I don't understand
Why you won't let me love you
Let me love you.
Alyson, I love you.

Shocked by the raw emotion, she looked away in time to see his bandmates both glance his way in surprise. This must not have been what they rehearsed.

Had he really said he loved her?

But they kept playing, and suddenly, she realized the melodies of the violin and the guitar had merged, that they played one tune, together. He had said he could only communicate through music. Twice now, he had merged them in song.

As the last high note held in the air, the gathered crowd began to clap and cheer. She looked around her—their audience had grown considerably.

He set the lyre in a padded box and strode toward her.

She swallowed, still stunned.

He leaned against the cash wrap, two feet of counter separating them.

"We can start with a date on Friday night. A real date. I've already got a babysitter." His grin was cool and collected, but his eyes begged as the grin began to falter.

"Say yes!" someone in the crowd yelled.

"All of this for a date?" She glanced around the department store, most of the crowd hanging on for whatever happened next.

Marcus hung his head and blew out loudly as if he'd been holding his breath. "I didn't mean to embarrass you."

"I've met your whole family, Marcus. You've sung lullabies to Andre, and you're Darius's hero. I think we might be beyond dating."

Had he really said he loved her?

"I agree." He held her gaze with a new intensity and took her hands in his. "Marry me."

"What?"

Barbara took her by the shoulders and walked her around the cash wrap to be with Marcus. She walked in a daze.

Was this really happening?

Marcus smiled at Barbara then took Alyson's hands again. For once, his hands were not warm.

"I thought I'd ask you about four months from now. Ask you to be my wife and come with me to California." He pulled her hands to his chest. "If you need something lasting to hold onto, let it be me, Alyson. Let it be me. I won't let you down. I promise."

He kissed the backs of her hands. "All those things you saw as limitations? Take another look at them from this perspective—they're *freedoms*. God's making it easy to walk away from this life, so that we can start a new one together."

And she saw it. The house selling out from under her, the job that would go nowhere but kept her from her children with long hours, her mother moving to California, her ex giving up custody of the boys—yes, now all those curses seemed blessings in this light. God had prepared the way, but she hadn't been able to see His plan.

And the biggest blessing was Marcus.

Marcus coming into their lives to rescue her son . . . and enliven her heart. Marcus who was the only one who really listened to what she meant, not just what she said. Marcus who had seen her at her worst again and again and somehow still liked her, even loved her. Marcus who cared more about awakening her spirit than he did about awakening her body.

She missed his smile when he wasn't near, missed his touch. Missed him.

Could a life together be possible? They'd only known each other a short time. Just like his parents, and his grandparents who'd had a fifty-year marriage.

She heard his grandmother's loving remembrance, talking about her beloved Milty and following him around the world after knowing him for only six weeks, "When you know, you just know."

"It's okay, you don't have to answer now. I know I surprised you. The fact you didn't say no is all the encouragement I need. That, and your beautiful smile."

And then she realized her cheeks hurt from smiling so big.

"Yes! Yes! A million times yes!" She jumped up and down, making a total spectacle of herself, and she didn't care who saw it.

Now it was his turn to be shocked. She laughed at the dumbfounded look on his face. She threw her arms around him and kissed him for every kind word and deed since she'd known him. The people around them clapped and cheered. The violinist played a jolly version of the wedding march.

Barbara hugged her, and Mr. Giles shook Marcus's hand. Was this really happening? She was buzzing and crying and laughing and it felt so right.

Together. They would tackle the future, *their future*, together.

With Marcus by her side, it would be an adventure.

A Note from the Author

Thank you so much for reading!
Enjoyed the book?
Please write a review on Amazon.
Independent authors don't have the marketing
budgets of the big publishing houses, so we depend
on our readers to help
spread the word about our books.
If you don't write a review, please share your
enjoyment of the book with all of your reader
friends. You could buy it for them as a gift and help
spread this message of love and faith.

Don't miss Book 2
in the Music of My Heart series:
Hollywood Heartbreak
Follow Marcus and Alyson to Hollywood and
witness the obstacles they face in starting a new life
together—nothing comes easily and what does come
may sear their souls.
Also—Will Gail reunite with her repentant ex-
husband? Or will she allow herself the new love she
never saw coming?
Don't miss this dual-storyline book!

Look for *Hollywood Heartbreak* in early 2019.

Go to www.SophiaIsaac.com for More
Download a FREE Book Club Guide
Download a FREE Recipe Booklet
Get to know the author
Join Sophia's newsletter for info on new releases

www.sophiaisaac.com

www.ingramcontent.com/pod-product-compliance
Lightning Source LLC
Chambersburg PA
CBHW070645180626
46817CB00006B/2245

* 9 7 8 1 9 4 9 7 3 0 0 1 2 *